FLIPPING NUMBERS 2
FRIENDS BECOME FOES

A novel

ERNEST MORRIS

Good2Go Publishing

This novel is a work of fiction. All the characters, organizations, establishments, and events portrayed in this novel are either product of the author's imagination or are fiction.

Published by:
GOOD2GO PUBLISHING
7311 W. Glass Lane
Laveen, AZ 85339
www.good2gopublishing.com
Twitter @good2gobooks
G2G@good2gopublishing.com
Facebook.com/good2gopublishing
ThirdLane Marketing: Brian James
Brian@good2gopublishing.com

Cover Design: Davida Baldwin
ISBN: 9780990869443

Acknowledgments

First and foremost, I would like to thank God for blessing me with this gift. Without you by my side, I would not have been able to make it through the many roadblocks and burdens that were placed against me. It is because of you that I have stayed strong and focused.

I would also like to thank Mr. and Mrs. Michael Lopez. You believed in me and stayed true and loyal, even when I doubted myself. Thank you both! That really meant a lot to me.

I dedicate this book to my late mother Jacqueline Morris and my late aunt Cathrine Heckstall. Even though you are gone, you continue to give me the strength that I need to make it in this cruel world.

To my children, Le`shea Burrell, Demina Johnson, Sa`meer and Shayana Morris, you loved me through all my wrong doings and never gave up on me, even when I left you alone in a corrupt world full of vultures, with just your mothers to guide you. Everything I do now is for you.

I would also like to thank and dedicate this book to a host of important people in my life, none more important than Yahnise Harmon. Through my whole incarnation, you have never left my side. Yahnise no matter what happens in my life; you will always have a place in my heart. To everybody else Dwunna, Kimyetta, Lyric, Jamie, Sedric, Kevin, Theresa, Loveana, Maurice, Rasheed, Frank, Rhonda, Lisa, Nyia, Chris, Nakisha, Brandi, Zarina, Tasha, Bo, Dee, Tysheeka, Barry, Laneek, Donnie, Dave, Tyreek, Scrap, Alisha, Tamara, Ed, etc…the list goes on and on. If I didn't mention you, I apologize.

Thank you everyone for supporting me.

PROLOGUE

Saturday night was cold as hell as everybody stayed in the house from the snow. The roads were closed due to the state of emergency warning that was broadcasted all over the T.V. and radio stations.

Tuck was sitting in his car with the heat on blast waiting for the perfect time to holla at the female he was waiting for. He had smoked two Dutches of Sour Diesel so he was in full street mode.

After waiting for an hour, the lights finally went out in the house he was watching. It was now 2:30 a.m. and he wanted to hurry up and get back home to his warm bed.

He took out his Glock, put the silencer on it, and then tucked it back in his waist. Tuck got out of the car and then pulled his skully down over his head. Then threw his hoodie on over the top of it.

He went across the street and cut through the alley heading towards the back door of the woman's crib. He climbed the fence, jimmied the lock on the window, and then slid into the house. Once he was inside, he took his gun out and took the safety off. Tuck started for the stairs when he noticed someone lying on the couch.

He walked up on the sleeping female and aimed his gun at her head.

PHHH!

PHHH!

PHHH!

Tuck put three rounds in her head. He then proceeded up the stairs towards the bedrooms and checked the first room, but it was empty.

He then walked towards the second room, but only came up empty again. When Tuck reached the master bedroom, he saw a figure lying on the top of the comforter. She wasn't wearing anything but a pair of black thongs. Her body was so beautiful that he almost had second thoughts about the situation. At the end of the day, he knew what he came to do so it had to get done.

He walked over to the bed and stared at the figure before him. Then he leaned over and smelled the Victoria Secret perfume all over her body. The smell from the perfume gave him an instant erection. Tuck took his finger and placed it between her legs feeling the heat radiating from her pussy. He knew he was wrong, but he had to have a taste of the victim before he killed her.

As Tuck went to move his finger, the woman's eyes opened causing him to panic. He aimed his gun at her while placing his other hand over her mouth.

"Shhhh! Don't fucking say a word or I will fucking kill you," he said to the woman. "Do you understand?"

She looked at him as if she was scared to death, but she mustered up enough strength to nod her head yes.

Tuck took his gun, placed it between her legs, and rubbed her pussy through her thong.

"Open your legs up wide," he said while still rubbing her pussy.

She was terrified so she did as she was told. He took the gun and pulled her thong to the side before shoving the gun inside of her.

She tried to scream from the pain, but he still had his hand over her mouth. Looking down at her in so much pain gave him a rush of adrenaline.

He didn't want to play anymore so he pulled the trigger while the gun was still inside of her

PHHH!

PHHH!

PHHH!

The shots killed her instantly, but he wasn't done yet.

Tuck took the hunting knife out of the case connected to his belt, leaned over towards the dead corpse, and cut her throat. Next, he pulled her tongue through her neck giving her a Columbian necktie. "That's what we do for rats! You fucking Puta!" he said as he headed out the room.

Tuck left out of the house the same way he came in. Once he was in his car, he took his gloves off and put them in a bag. He looked over to the house and said, "That should teach all of you fucking snitches a lesson." Then he started his car and left the scene of the crime.

* * *

Monday afternoon, EJ was sitting in his cell listening to his Walkman when he heard the Correctional Officer (C/O) walking around passing out mail. When she approached his cell, she said, "Johnson, Reed, you both have mail." She passed EJ and his celi their mail and kept it moving. EJ seen the cover of the newspaper he had received, but he didn't really pay it any attention. He looked at the letter from his lawyer and opened it up.

When EJ read the contents of the letter, his heart felt like it was about to fall out of his chest. He couldn't believe what he was reading. It took him a minute to reread the letter. After reading it over again, reality hit him. He dropped the letter and anxiously picked the newspaper back up. He immediately read the article on the front page. That's as far as he could go before the tears started flowing down his face like a waterfall.

"OH MY GOD! WHAT HAVE I DONE?" he said out loud, as he covered his face.

EJ's celi jumped off his bed to see what was wrong. "What happened?" he asked grabbing the paper out of EJ's hands and reading the front page. The headline read, *"Two Female Bodies Were Found in a Southwest Philly House Yesterday Morning Shot Multiple Times."*

Scrap looked at his celi and said, "E, what's going on? You know them?" EJ looked up at his celi and shook his head as the tears continued to flow.

CHAPTER 1

Locked Down

EJ was sitting in his cell trying to come up with an explanation about why all this took place. He couldn't figure out why his stepmom would not only snitch him out, but also her own flesh and blood. There had to be a reason this had happened, but he would never be able to know because she was dead. the thought of her being dead brought tears to his eyes again. What really hurt him was the fact that he was the one who had ordered the hit. If only he would have waited on the paperwork. Then he could have come up with a different option. As much as he hated snitching, he might have given her a pass.

Just as all the thoughts were flustering his brain, someone tapped on his cell door. When he looked over, he spotted Juan standing there. "Come in man," EJ said as he moved his Walkman off the bed so Juan could sit down.

Once Juan sat down he said, "Man this is some crazy shit that happened. Ed ain't taking it too good either. He wants to know who put the hit out on his mom. He knows you didn't do it because you always leave shit up to him."

EJ listened to Juan, trying to think of something to say. Juan worked as a barber and he had left the hole from cutting some inmates hair. He was talking to Ed and he had told him to see if EJ had the scoop yet. Ed couldn't wait to get out of the hole so that he could get on the phone and find the answers that he was looking for.

He knew EJ was on it, that's why he sent a message to him. They wouldn't let E go to his mom's funeral because his bail was too high.

EJ knew no one could ever find out about this so he acted as if he didn't know shit. "I'm still trying to find out what happened and as soon as I do, we will handl it," EJ said to Juan.

"At least something good may come out of this if they drop the charges. H may have lost his mom and it's a shame, but a snitch is a snitch," Juan said. "If yo ask me, I think she got what she des—."

Before he could get the rest of the word out, EJ had jumped up and grabbe Juan around his throat. "Don't you even think about finishing that statement nigga! don't want to hear anything negative come out of your mouth about her again," E said letting Juan go so he could catch his breath.

Juan looked at EJ and he knew he meant business. Usually he would fuck an nigga up that stepped to him, but he had seen something in EJ's eyes that made hin think twice about it. "My bad man. I didn't mean any disrespect by that. I hate whe niggas run their mouth to get themselves out of trouble. Nobody lives by the code o the streets anymore," Juan said rubbing his throat.

"I know man, my bad. I'm bugging right now from this shit. Do you wan something to drink?" EJ asked grabbing two sodas out of his box.

"Naw, I'm good. I have to go get in the shower before they call count. Oh before I go, Ed wanted me to give you this letter," Juan said passing the note to EJ.

"Alright, get up with me later on so we can talk about some shit. If you see m celi out there, tell him I said don't come up yet cause I'm about to take a shit," E said getting up and giving Juan a pound.

"Alright. I'll hit you later," he said leaving the room.

EJ sat on his bunk and opened up the letter that Ed had sent him.

What's good Cannon,

As you can see from reading the paper, and watching on the news, my mom wa murdered. I'm stuck in this hole and can't even find out anything. I really need yo to find out what happened. I need to know who killed my mom, man. I'm going thr it in this joint. I can't wait to get out of this hole. Then on top of it, they won't let m go to her funeral. I know you're going to make sure that Erica gives her a prope funeral so I'm not worried about that. Where do that leave this case? Did you holl at Savino yet? Let me know by sending me a kite back with Juan. My nigga sta strong because we're not going to let these mutha fuckers get away with this. We have to find out who ordered the hit. I think it was Wan's bitch ass. I never liked him anyway. Well, be safe and I'll see you soon.

One Love,

Ed

After reading the kite that Ed sent, EJ could only feel even guiltier. He had to try to make things right with his friend, but he didn't know how. He decided to wait and see how everything unfolded.

* * *

The next day, Savino had come to talk with EJ. They were sitting in the official's visiting booth. "I told you to wait until I sent you the affidavit before you made a move. Now what do you want me to do?" Savino asked.

"I want you to get us the fuck out of here. That shouldn't be an issue now that the star witness is out of the way; right?" EJ asked looking at Savino.

"Well my team is working on that as we speak, but you have to be patient because they still have enough evidence to go to trial. We're going to argue the fact that it shouldn't be admissible without the star witness. So let me work on that. We have a hearing next week and you and your whole team should be set free," Savino said as he gathered the papers up and put them in his briefcase.

A smile came across EJ's face as he thought about going home to his wife. He wanted to wrap his arms around Yahnise's beautiful body again. He couldn't wait until his next visit because he had paid a C/O to let him slide in a bathroom with his wife. The C/O told him to pay him five hundred dollars and she would work the visiting room that day so he could do it. He told his wife to bring the money with her when she came.

"Okay, well guess I'll see you next week in court then," EJ said as he stood up, shook Savino's hand and walked out the door.

Before EJ could leave Savino questioned, "Will everything be alright between you and Ed?"

"As long as he never knows I ordered the hit on his mom," he said and then shut the door behind him.

* * *

Ed was sitting in his cell thinking about all the possible suspects that could have ordered the hit. He knew only two people could get ahold of the affidavit so fast. That was Wan and EJ. He didn't really think that his friend would do something like that, but Wan probably would. Once they got out of here though, he was going to find out who killed his mom and make them pay.

Ed had talked to his lawyer today also and found out that they all had a court hearing scheduled for next week. He knew he would get the chance to see everybody and he would see who looked guilty or not.

Ed picked up the picture of his mom and stared at it. She looked so beautiful standing there with him and Tamara at their wedding. "Mom when I find the person who killed you, I'm going to cut their head off and feed it to the sharks," he said as tears came down his face. He cried for two reasons. One because she was gone forever and two because she really wanted him in jail. He couldn't get over the fact that his mom was a rat.

He took one last look at the picture before ripping it up and flushing it down the toilet. In his right mind, he knew that it had to be done to save his freedom, but he thought that the decision should have been his to make, not an outsider.

The slot of the door suddenly opened up taking Ed out of his dangerous thoughts. A female C/O by the name of Ms. Watson passed Ed his dinner through the slot. She was average with nice size chest and a round shaped ass. She wore her hair down with a hat. She never worked the hole so it surprised Ed when he seen her.

"What you doing working down here? Don't you belong in Central Control pushing buttons or something? Ed asked with a smirk.

"Keep it up Mr. Young and you won't get another chance to push this button anymore," she said seductively.

Ed and Ms. Watson had been fucking off and on when he was home. She was one of his jump-offs that he frequently visited whenever he and Tamara would argue. She never once mentioned his wife's name and she never got attached.

What Ed didn't know was that she was one of the females in the prison that would fuck you if the price were right. She never told him because she wanted him to approach her about it first. She knew that if he asked her, she would willingly do it, but she wanted to see what kind of profit she would get from it.

"How long are you going to be over here?" Ed asked looking at his food to see what they had served him tonight.

"Until 11 o'clock. Why? What do you need mister?" she said with her hand on her hips.

Ed looked to see if anyone was paying them any attention. When he saw that no one was, he put his hand through the slot and rubbed her pussy causing her panties to moisten. "I want some of this wet-wet right here. I've been trying to catch you alone since I've been here. So can you make it happen or what?" he said still rubbing her pussy.

"What's in it for me if I do?" she questioned while opening her legs up a little as he kept rubbing through the fabric of her uniform.

"I'll make sure that you are well compensated for this so is it a go or do I have to do it myself like I've been doing?" Ed said smirking.

Ms. Watson looked around and then put her hand through the slot and grabbed Ed's dick. "I will be back at 10:30. That gives us fifteen minutes so don't be taking all long. I'm not trying to lose my job for no one; you understand?" she said seriously.

Ed moved away and said," I'll be waiting." He went over and sat on his bunk to eat his food. He couldn't wait to fuck Keira (Ms. Watson) like he use to when he was home. He knew once they started, she wouldn't want him to stop.

After he ate, he was going to take a nap so that he would be fully charged when she got back. It was only 5 p.m. so he had plenty of time. Besides, he needed that stress reliever to take his mind off of everything else.

* * *

It was 10:33 p.m. and Keira still wasn't there yet. Ed was getting frustrated because he thought that she would have been there by now. He started thinking that something else came up when he heard footsteps approaching. Ed jumped up and waited for whoever was coming to stop at the door.

When the door opened, Keira wasn't the one standing there. It was a white Sargent named McBride. She looked at Ed in his boxers and couldn't take her eyes off of his erection. She finally looked up and said, "I'm Sargent McBride and Ms. Watson couldn't make it so she sent me. They are shaking a unit down upstairs and it could be a while."

Ed looked at the think white snow bunny and said, "Well come on in."

She came in and pulled the door a little. She didn't want the other inmates to hear anything. She walked over to the bunk and pulled her pants down. "Take it easy; okay. This is my first time with a black guy," she said while sticking her finger in her already wet pussy.

Ed quickly pulled his dick out and bent Ms. McBride over the bed. When he put the head in, she screamed out in ecstasy. "Oh my God! That shit feels so fucking good! Tear this pussy up baby!" she said as she spread her legs open and put her head in the pillow to muffle the sound.

Ed started ramming her pussy like it was no tomorrow. "Yeah baby, take this dick. You feel so good, fuck," he said, as he was already getting ready to bust.

Ms. McBride's body was like Kaley Cuoco from *"The Big Bang Theory."* She had a tattoo of a dragon that went around her body and came up her leg blowing fire into her pussy. That shit had Ed ready to start thinking her shit was hot. He laughed it off and said to himself, *"As good as this pussy is, I don't mind getting burnt."*

"Ummmm Daddy… I'm about to cum. Keep hitting my spot like that," she said as she started throwing it back.

Ed nor Ms. McBride couldn't take it any longer and both of them simultaneously climaxed together. Ms. McBride pulled her pants back up and fixed her uniform. She walked out the cell and shut the door without even saying anything.

Ed stood there with his dick in his hand looking stupid. "What the fuck happened?" he said to no one in particular.

He shook his head and started taking a birdbath to wash the smell of sex off of him. He couldn't wait until he got out of the hole so he could get up with both of them. One thing was for certain, he was going to get him so more of Ms. McBride.

CHAPTER 2

Good News

"Johnson, get ready for court. They'll be here to get you in twenty minutes," the C/O said waking EJ up from his sleep. They had finally received a date back in court to determine if the proceedings will go on or if they would be going home. EJ laid there thinking about what might happen once they set foot in the courtroom. Even if he didn't get out, he hoped that at least his crew was released. Ever since they had been locked up, they hadn't made any kind of money. All of their bank accounts had been frozen except their offshore accounts.

EJ was glad that he had opened them because that's how his wife and son have been living since the arrest. She would wire money into her sister Nyia's account and then withdraw it. They didn't have to worry about anything because there was no connection that linked them to any kind of wrongdoing. He wanted all this to go away and hopefully today would be that day.

He got up to brush his teeth and wash his face. Scrap was already up getting ready to go to work in the kitchen. "Yo, so it might be over today, huh?" he said putting on his shoes.

"Yeah, I sure hope so because I need to get money. I've grown accustomed to a certain lifestyle and I want to continue living that way," EJ said brushing his teeth.

"So you think they will try to do some backdoor shit to y'all?" Scrap asked.

EJ looked at Scrap and said, "They will try to do anything to keep a nigg down, but my lawyer is ready for whatever they bring," he said confidently.

"That's what I want to hear. Good luck and whatever happens don't let destroy who you are. From what I see, you are a man of honor and integrity. Th speaks volumes in my book," Scrap said.

"Thanks man and like I told you, when you get out, look me up for a job. I ca use someone like you on my team. Once all this shit blows over, there will be a l of niggas trying to take down the empire that we will be building. I refuse to let th shit happen," EJ said brushing his hair.

"I appreciate the offer and I'll think it over when the time is right," Scrap sa leaving the cell.

After EJ was finished getting ready, he went up to the front of the block an waited to go handle his business. Regardless of what happens today, he was goin to come out of it a winner. He made a promise to himself that if they proceeded wit the case, he would take the fall so that everyone else could go home.

EJ knew Yahnise wouldn't approve of it, so he told her to stay at home. H couldn't stand to see the disappointment in her eyes if something went wrong. N matter what she said, he made up an excuse. He hoped that it worked.

* * *

The CJC courtroom was crowded. Everybody came to support EJ and his cre hoping to see some justice done. The judge that would be presiding over the cas was Judge Means. Everybody had different opinions of him and they all weren good ones.

EJ and Wan were waiting in the back when Ed walked in the courtroom. The all shared a brotherly hug. Ed gave Wan a bit of a cold shoulder. Until he found o what happened to his mother, he was the one person of interest.

They had Shannon and Tiffany over in the woman's holding cell. Everybod had on brand new dress clothes courtesy of Yahnise and Tamara. They had broug them up a couple of days before so they could look presentable when they went i front of the judge.

"How are you holding up man? I was worried about you ever since I heard th news. I still can't believe that she's gone," EJ said pacing the floor.

"I'm hanging in there for now. I can't wait to get out of here so we can get to the bottom of this. They must have forced my mom to do the shit she did. She wouldn't snitch on none of us like that," Ed said looking at the wall.

"Are you sure about that? She was on that shit," Wan said staring at Ed.

In one quick motion, Ed punched Wan dead in the face. Wan fell on the bench, but jumped back up ready for war. EJ jumped in between the two of them trying to calm the situation down before it got out of hand.

"Chill the fuck out man. It's nobody's fault in here. We have to stay strong and get through this as a team," EJ said. Then he looked over to Wan, "That was some foul shit to say. Keep your comments to yourself."

"For all we know, this nigga is the one that ordered the fucking hit," Ed said wanting to get at Wan.

"I would never do that shit. I apologize for coming off like that. I shouldn't have said that," Wan said trying to calm down.

They both went on opposite sides of the holding cell. EJ wanted to tell his friend the truth, but it wasn't the time or place to air out any dirty laundry. His conscience was eating him up inside and he didn't know how much longer he could go without telling someone. For now though, he would keep it inside.

The Sheriff came to the cell and looked at his clipboard. "Eric Johnson, Edward Young, and Wan Lee, please come with me. The judge is ready to see you," he said as he opened the cell.

The Sheriff then escorted them to the elevator and took them to the fifth floor. When they got to the fifth floor, they were then placed in a holding room until it was time to go in.

EJ was thinking about all types of different scenarios that could happen, but he didn't want to say anything yet.

"Well fellas, it's us against them out there. As long as we stay together, we should be all right. If it don't look like it's going in our favor, then I will take the hit so that y'all can go home," EJ said to his friends.

"What the hell are you talking about? We are in this shit together. If you go down, then I go with you," Ed said looking at EJ as if he had lost his mind.

"You don't understand. You have a fam—..." EJ said before being cut off.

"And so do you nigga. I can't speak for everybody else, but it's not going down like that," Ed said.

"I agree with him on this EJ. That's crazy," Wan said.

Before EJ could respond, the Sheriff opened the door letting them know it was that time. As they walked into the courtroom, it was obvious how many people were on their side. Everybody was in attendance. Tamara, Tuck, EJ's aunt Bobby, Erica, Nyia, Ms. Pam, Chris, Mira, Ziaire, and Yahnise. That was only half of the support they had.

When EJ saw Yahnise, he didn't know what to do. She whispered, "I love you" to him and he said it back. He should have known that she wouldn't stay home. All and all, he was happy that she was there, but he hoped that it stayed that way.

"All rise," the bailiff said as the judge made his entrance. Everyone stood up and waited for the judge to instruct them.

"You may be seated," he said. He then turned and looked at the clerk and asked, "What is our first case on the docket?"

The clerk looked at the paper and said, "The first case Your Honor is Commonwealth verses Eric Johnson, Edward Young, Wan Lee, Shannon Clark, and Tiffany Green."

EJ saw the female bailiff escort Tiffany and Shannon into the courtroom. As soon as they saw him and the rest of their crew, they smiled. They all nodded as they came and stood next to EJ. The whole Savino firm was in attendance. They stood up and stated their names and whom they were representing.

When EJ looked over to the Defense Attorney (DA) side, he saw Agent Kaplin and Detective Harris sitting there with smirks on their faces. He wanted to go over there and beat the shit down their legs, but he controlled his anger.

"Alright, let's get this hearing underway," the judge said. He looked over to the DA. "Will the state please state your facts?"

The Deputy District Attorney stood up and began talking about all of the evidence that they had on them. "Your Honor, the state ask that you not dismiss these charges because of the severity of the crimes. We have wiretaps, computer equipment that was confiscated from numerous houses, and defendants collecting money from different houses. We had a witness that was ready and willing to testify, but was killed in a home invasion. The good thing is we still have her statement," the DA said as she held up the papers in her hand.

"We also have the two leading officers in this case here willing to testify on behalf of the state. We cannot let these people go free. They are a part of an organized crime family involving money laundering, aggravated ID theft, fraud, criminal conspiracy, and the list goes on and on. It is up to the court to make sure that these types of crimes don't go unpunished," the DA said trying to paint a negative picture for the judge.

EJ listened to the DA go on and on with her speech. He couldn't believe all the information they had. He wanted to know how much more Ms. Cynthia had told them before the raids and her demise. He knew that his lawyer would fight fire with fire so he wasn't worried not one bit.

Judge Means listened to the DA's opening statements and once she was done, he looked over to the defense table, "Counselors are you ready for your statements?"

Louis Savino stood up and looked at the judge. "Your Honor, all the evidence that the state has is all coming from a witness that is deceased. Without her testimony and written statement, they don't have a case. I'm asking you to dismiss all charges on those grounds alone. How can you even think about proceeding with this case without circumstantial evidence?" he asked as he stood near the desk. when he was about to continue, his paralegal walked through the door. She came up and passed him a piece of paper. Savino studied the paper and then looked over to the prosecutor's with a sinister look on his face.

Savino turned and looked at his partners as well as all of his clients and smiled while showing them the paperwork that he had received. Then he gave it to the DA to read. Her face turned red as she passed the paper back to Savino who then gave it to the judge before he spoke.

"Your Honor in light of the new evidence, I ask that this case be thrown out due to the fact that of the cops involved," he said turning towards Agent Kaplin and Detective Harris who were wondering what happened. "Compromised the whole case by not obtaining a warrant to search the premises of a Southwest Philadelphia home," he continued.

The judge finished reading the document that was passed to him and then gave it back to the bailiff to pass it back to Savino. He looked at the prosecution side and shook his head in disgrace.

He then took his glasses off and leaned back in his chair. "You had this robust, intense criminal investigation and you sacrificed the integrity of that investigation and the ability of it to get to its goal by being placed in an inexcusable situation.

You should have gotten a warrant to search the premises at 2228 South 56th Street. So for that, I have no choice, but to drop all the charges against the defendants. Maybe next time those officers will follow the proper protocol and get a warrant. Case dismissed. Next case, please," Judge Means said sounding disappointed.

The spectators went crazy. Yahnise and Tamara started crying and hugging each other as they seen their men being led out by the Sheriff. They were tears of joy because they knew they would be with their husbands by the end of the night.

Savino shook EJ's hand and said, "I told you I had a trick up my sleeve. I had my assistant contact the courts to see if any of the warrants were valid for the houses. When they told her they couldn't find one on the Southwest residence, she got suspicious and did some more research. She found out that they never got a warrant so everything had to be thrown out. Even with the eyewitness, they still had no case. You and your friends should be home by dinner. I'll make sure of that," Savino said.

"You are one bad man," EJ said smiling at his attorney. That smile faded when he thought about what he had said. That means he didn't have to order that hit that killed Ed's mom. He really felt like shit now. He decided that it was best to never tell his friend what really happened. He also hoped that he didn't' find out.

* * *

EJ was in his cell waiting for them to call his name for discharge. He couldn't wait to hit the streets. "Come on man. I need a partner to play spades. I'll split the money with you. Plus you need to be doing something until they call you," Scrap said standing in the door.

Just as EJ was about to go, they called his name to pack up. "Damn baby-boy, it's time to get the fuck up outta here," EJ said grabbing his mail.

"Yo, don't forget about me when I come home. I'll be out in a month," Scrap said shaking EJ's hand.

"Man get at me when your bitch ass gets home. I left you over two hundred dollars in commissary so you should be good until you gamble it all away," EJ said with a smirk on his face. "If you need anything, call my cell phone. Niggas know you cool with me so nobody will try and come at you."

"Alright nigga be safe and I'll see you when I touch. I have to go back to Delaware, but I'll be on the next thing smoking back out this way to see you," Scrap said as EJ left out the cell.

When EJ got to the receiving room, he saw Wan, but not Ed. "Where is Ed at?" EJ asked Wan.

"I don't know. They don't even have his street clothes out with ours," Wan said looking up at the bags on the rack.

"We have to find out why they didn't let him out yet," EJ said putting his street clothes on.

Once they collected all of their valuables, they headed out the door. As soon as they reached the gate, family and friends were all there to greet them. Yahnise ran and jumped into EJ's arms. They kissed passionately before he released her.

"Where is my little man at?" he asked hugging his wife.

"Over there with my mom in the car sleep," she said excited.

Tamara was looking around for Ed and she was disappointed when she didn't see him. She went over to where EJ and Yahnise were standing. "Where is my boo?" she asked looking sad.

EJ gave her a hug and said, "He still in there, but I'm going to find out right now why he didn't come out with us."

EJ walked over to where Savino was talking to his colleagues. When Savino looked up he said, "Welcome home, my friend. Before you say anything, we are trying to get Mr. Young out now. They are still holding him on that gun charge. Most likely we can have him out in a couple of weeks."

EJ sighed. "Okay, but do what you can so his wife can see him sooner if possible," he said shaking his head.

"What are you going to do about that other situation?" Savino questioned EJ.

"It will be taken care of. Let's get back to business tomorrow. Tonight I'm going home to sleep in my bed with my wife. When will we have access to our bank accounts again?" EJ said.

"They should be up and running by tomorrow afternoon. Beings though they dropped all the charges, they can no longer keep the freeze on the accounts," Savino said walking away towards his car.

EJ nodded his head as he went back over towards his wife and Tamara. He told her the news about Ed and then they left for their houses. EJ couldn't wait to make love to his wife. It had been a while so they had a lot of catching up to do. Tomorrow though, he would be putting his new plan into motion. He was a wealthy man and he was determined to stay that way by any means necessary.

CHAPTER 3

Back to Business

EJ was in his Bentley on his way to see a friend that he met a year ago. He never thought that he would be contacting him, but it was time to turn it the fuck up in the streets.

He pulled up in the WaWa parking lot on Route 13 in New Castle, Delaware. As soon as he parked, he spotted whom he had come to see. He exited the car and walked over to the Chrysler 300. The driver unlocked the passenger door and EJ slid in.

"I see you still driving your mom's shit. When are you going to buy your own car and I hope you at least moved into your own crib," EJ said giving the man pound (handshake).

Loud Pack laughed at the remarks before saying, "I do have my own crib now and this is my shit. I put it in her name to keep those pigs off of my back."

"That's your story and you're sticking to it; right," EJ said as they both shared laugh before discussing business.

Loud Pack whose real name was Donnie supplied all of the Delaware and some parts of Maryland with loud. That's where he got his name. He was originally from Philly, but he moved out to Delaware with his mom to get away from the bullshit there. He started selling a little bit of loud here and there and he eventually blew up

The demand was so high for the shit that he had to start copping weight.

After about three months, Loud Pack was dealing straight with the connect. Then he stared supplying him with Mollies and a little bit of dope. Loud Pack didn't know anything about dope so he didn't want too much of it. He had talked to EJ and Ed about the dope game before they were booked. Now he was going to introduce EJ to his connect.

"Well I talked to Pedro last night and he would like to do business with you," Loud Pack said.

"That's why I'm here. I need to get my hands on some pure shit. I want the best product in the tristate area. When will he be ready to meet because time is money and I don't like wasting either," EJ said to Loud Pack.

"We are on our way to meet him now. He will be waiting for us at the West Inn Hotel over on the riverfront. You can either follow me or you can ride with me," Loud Pack said.

EJ laughed at him before saying, "I think I'll be following you. I don't want to get caught slipping in your mom's wheels."

"Go ahead with that shit. This is my car and mine only," Loud Pack said getting defensive.

"Whatever you say man. Lead the way and I'll follow you because I don't know where I'm going," EJ said as he got out of Loud Pack's car and jumped back into his Bentley.

* * *

About five minutes later, they pulled up to the West Inn. It wasn't even open yet because they were still building it. As they pulled over, EJ noticed a limo and two GMC Yukons flicking their lights. Loud Pack got out of the care and walked over to EJ's car.

"Okay, my man Pedro is in the limo waiting for you. I'll sit here and wait for you while y'all conduct business," Loud Pack said as EJ got out of his car.

"Why you didn't tell me that this mutha-fucka was still under construction," EJ asked sounding a little angry.

"This is where we have always met ever since I have been dealing with him. He don't like being around a lot of people conducting business. He's cool. I can vouch for him. He said the same about you," Loud Pack smirked.

EJ thought about it for a minute. It did make sense to do business in a discrete location. He walked over towards the limo as two men jumped out of the Yukon. They stopped EJ before he got to the car. They searched him for a weapon and then opened the limo so he could get in.

When he got in the limo, he seen a Spanish man that looked no older than forty years of age. "Hello, my friend. My name is Pedro and it's nice to meet you," he said shaking EJ's hand. "Would you like something to drink," he asked pouring some Louis XIII in his glass.

"No thanks. I don't drink," EJ said.

"You're a smart man. Once you start, it's hard to stop," Pedro said sipping on his drink. "So I hear you are looking to buy some weight in large quantities. Can you move that much beings though this not the type of business you're usually involved in?"

Pedro noticed the look of surprise on EJ's face. "Yes, Mr. Eric Johnson, twenty-three years old, wife, and son. I do my homework before I deal with anybody new. I know you came home yesterday. You were locked up for check fraud, but beat it due to an illegal search and seizure. You and your partner had a couple of blocks pumping small time weight, but this is the big league right here. Are you sure you are ready? I hope you are not biting off more than you can chew," Pedro said.

"I'm not a little kid anymore so yes I can handle this," EJ said taking off his Tom Ford sunglasses.

"So tell me, how much do you wish to purchase at this time?" Pedro asked putting his glass down.

"I would like to cop maybe two bricks for now," EJ said to Pedro.

Pedro looked at EJ and smirked. He was shocked at what he heard. "That's all you want? As I said before, you are in the big leagues now. I don't sell less than ten a pop. I'll tell you what I can do though. If you buy at least five bricks at $40,000.00 a brick, I will give you another five bricks on consignment. Off of the extra five I give you, I want $150,000.00 back. That means that I'm giving you the extra five bricks for $30,000.00 apiece. So you'll pay me $200,000.00 up front and the rest later when you need to re-up. This is a deal of a lifetime so take it or leave it," Pedro said.

He was throwing numbers around like a human calculator. At the same time, so was EJ. off that one shipment, he would make more money than he could imagine.

The question that was going through his head was, where would he off it at... He could turn one key into seven easily.

His mind was made up. Even if he had to be out there all day, he wasn't turning this deal down. A brick would cost him $80,000.00 a pop, but he was getting five for only $200,000.00. He had no other choice, but to take it. "I'll take it," EJ said shaking Pedro's hand.

"When will you be ready to make the transaction?" Pedro asked.

"I'm ready now. I have $160,000.00 in my car and I can get the other $40,000.00 from the closest TD Bank here," EJ said excited.

"My driver can take us over to Market Street. There is a TD Bank over there. By the time we get back, your product will be in your car waiting for you," Pedro said.

"Give me one minute," EJ said stepping out of the limo and running over to his trunk. He took out the bag with the money and walked over to Loud Pack.

"Hold this until I come back. That's a lot of money so be careful," EJ said and then went over and got back in the limo.

"Let's go get your bread Mr. Pedro," EJ said sitting back rubbing his hands together.

* * *

An hour later EJ and Loud Pack were sitting in Loud Pack's mom house talking. His mom wasn't there so they could talk without whispering.

"I told you this would be a great deal for us. I know a few cats out in B-More who are looking for some weight. After we cut one or two of them, we can deliver them to whomever," Loud Pack said.

"Give those niggas a call and tell them we have those things for sale. I'm going to head back to Philly. I have to get me a couple of girls that don't mind cutting this up for me. I know who to call," EJ said as he was heading out the door with the bag containing the ten bricks.

"Are you coming or are you staying here at your mom's crib," EJ asked laughing because he knew he was getting under Loud Pack's skin.

"Yeah, yeah, yeah! I heard it all before. Let's go get us some naked women to put to work," he said sounding excited.

* * *

Loud Pack and EJ were over on the one hundred block of Millick Street with three girls that they knew. EJ had called Sharrell and her sister Jonay and Loud Pack had called some shorty by the name of Felicia from down the bottom (West Philly).

Sharrell and Jonay were both light skin beauties. EJ met them when he was down on 42nd and Westminister. Sharrell was about a dollar and Jonay was trying to follow after her big sister.

Felicia was from 39th and Mellon. She was brown skin and her body would put any model so shame. She had every nigga in West Philly in the palm of her hands. She wanted more so that she could always look out for her family.

EJ made them all a proposition that they couldn't refuse. All they had to do was come over every day and cut the dope with Banita and Quad 9, to turn one into seven. It was that simple. They would make $500.00 a day for only a couple of hours of work. Now he had them in the kitchen handling their business with nothing on but a pair of thongs. That was one of EJ's stipulations and they all agreed.

EJ didn't want anybody stealing from him. He didn't even know how to cut it so he relied on Loud Pack to show the girls what to do. This is where he missed his friend Ed. He would have been able to handle everything without any problems.

As they watched the girls handle their business, they talked about their next move. "My connect in B-More wants to cop eight at a time. He said he moves a brick every two days where he's at," Loud Pack said.

"That right there alone will have us sitting nice. We'll be rich within a month. All we have to do is sit back and collect the proceeds," EJ said smiling.

EJ watched the girls strut around the kitchen singing with the rap videos that were playing on the Plasma and surround sound. He kept watching Felicia wondering why he never paid her any attention when he lived on the block with his aunt. To him back then, she was like his little sister. Now she's all grown up and he couldn't deny how well she had transformed. She had nice perky titties, a flat stomach, and an ass that would make Beyoncé's look small. He felt an attraction to her, but he said he would never mix business with pleasure again especially after what had happened with Erica.

"I'm going to get something to eat. Do y'all want something?" EJ asked the girls.

"Yes, we are starving," Sharrell said removing her mask.

"Okay, I'll bring something from the pizza store down the street. Matter of fact, Felicia come roll with me," EJ said waiting for her to throw her clothes on.

Felicia put her skirt and shirt on and then grabbed her coat. They both headed out the door to EJ's car.

"Don't be taking all day to come back," Loud Pack said smirking because he knew EJ kept looking at Felicia's body.

"We won't be long dad," EJ said as he jumped in the car and pulled off.

As they drove to the pizza store on 57th and Spruce, EJ noticed Felicia kept looking at him. "What are you looking at, bighead?" he asked glancing over in her direction.

"I'm trying to figure out how someone who said they would never touch drugs is all of a sudden knee deep in it?" she questioned.

EJ smiled and said, "Oh so you remember all that shit I used to preach, huh?"

"Yeah and you used to always call me your sister. Now you got me all up in your house naked cutting dope. I know you be watching this forbidden fruit," she said as her hands moved up and down her body.

EJ shook his head. "You got that right; forbidden fruit!"

"Shut up boy! You're stupid," she said laughing. "Thank you for letting me do this for you and you won't have to worry about me taking anything from you."

EJ nodded his head as they parked to pick up the food. Felicia was leaned back in her seat. As EJ got out the car, he wondered what it would feel like in between her legs. He laughed and shook his head as he went in the store.

* * *

It was almost 9 p.m. when the girls were done cutting up five keys. EJ now had thirty-five keys sitting on the table. His eyes were big as hell because he had never seen so much dope in his life. Loud Pack had finished wrapping the last one up.

"We will do five more tomorrow. Call us when you are ready," Sharrell said as she put her shirt on and fastened her pants.

"Wait. We have to come up with a name so I can give it our signature stamp," EJ said to everybody.

"How about *Black Knight*," Jonay said.

"Hold up. I know. Let's call it *Withdraw*," Sharrell said.

They all looked at her as if she was crazy. Then everybody burst out laughing. She sat on the couch with her arms folded. They were trying to come up with a name for ten more minutes when Felicia snapped her fingers.

"I know what we can call it. Let's call it *Numbers*! The reason I say that is

because when we start flipping numbers, we will actually be flipping the dope," sh
said waiting for a response.

They all thought about it for a minute and then everybody started nodding thei
heads in agreement. "I like it," Loud Pack said.

"Well, by this time tomorrow we will have numbers all over the streets. Let'
get the hell up out of here. Loud Pack will drop you ladies off at home. I have t
jump on the highway and get home to my wife and little man. I'll see y'all her
tomorrow around noon," EJ said giving the girls a hug and Loud Pack a pound.

EJ couldn't wait to get his product on the streets. It was time to take over an
nothing was going to stop him.

CHAPTER 4

Plotting Revenge

E d had come from his visit with Tamara. He had only been out of the hole for a day so he made sure his wife came up. As he went to his cell, he noticed that someone new had come on the block. When he seen who it was, he walked over to his cell.

"Yo nigga, what's popping," he said to his friend Tuck.

"Oh shit! No they didn't put me over here with you," Tuck said giving Ed a pound.

They sat in Tuck's room talking for about an hour. Tuck had gotten snatched up for an ounce of weed. He knew he would be home in a day or two, so he really wasn't sweating it. He was waiting for his no good ass girl to handle everything.

"I hope Kia dumb ass post my bail today. She be on some bullshit when it comes to spending money," Tuck said.

"That's because you are always spoiling her with gifts. Now that you are here, she can't get that luxury she so used to. If she don't post it by tonight, I'll call EJ and he will have you out tomorrow," Ed said.

"I have money at home. My blocks are doing numbers right now. Before I got knocked yesterday, I heard that your man was starting to blow up with the dope game. He got a couple of niggas out of state pumping that shit and he dealing with a big time connect," Tuck said.

Ed was listening to all the shit Tuck was saying and wondering if it was true or not. EJ hadn't said anything about that when he talked to him on the phone. He thought that maybe it was because the calls were recorded.

"Damn, so my boy finally stepped up to the plate and hit a homerun, huh? I know he can't wait to tell me all about it. I'll be home in two weeks and we'll be getting money together again," Ed said.

"Yeah, y'all will have shit on smash when you get home. Nobody wants to go against you and EJ. Niggas really look up to the both of you and half of them wish they were y'all," Tuck said as he got up out of the chair. "I'm going to take a shower before my boo gets here to bail me out. I will come to your hut (cell) afterwards so we can bust it up some more."

Ed got up to walk out the door. "You're a sucker for love ass nigga," he said laughing at Tuck.

Tuck shook his head and hollered, "At least I'm not married, yet!"

Ed walked out of Tuck's cell and went straight over to the phone. He wanted to call EJ and make sure he knew what he was doing. After he made his call, he was going to holler at Ms. Watson or Sargent McBride. He had been fucking both of them ever since that night Sargent McBride came to his cell. He told them to call EJ when they left work and he would break them off for their troubles.

Once Ed called EJ three times only to get his voicemail, he left a quick message saying he needed to see him. He then went to the officer's desk to try to get in the hallway. "Aye, C/O White, I need to go to medical for a breathing treatment," Ed said because he knew he would get out that way.

"Okay Mr. Young, go get your Department of Corrections (DOC) shirt and head on over," C/O White said.

Ed grabbed his shirt and walked over to medical. When he got there, it wasn't anyone there except Ms. Watson. She was on the computer playing Solitaire. When she looked up and seen Ed, a smile came across her face.

"What do you want Mr. Young? You know that medical is closed until after count," she said.

"Well call my C/O on the block and tell them that I will be here during count getting my breathing treatment," Ed said taking a seat.

Ms. Watson looked at him with a seductive look on her face. "Well you are only getting some head because my period is on right now and it don't go off until tomorrow," she said while calling his housing unit to inform the officer that Ed would be there for the count.

"If it goes off tomorrow, that means you are only spotting. I'm not scared to run any red lights (have sex while a woman is on her period) anyway," Ed whispered to her while she was on the phone.

When she hung up the phone, she told him to follow her into ono of the rooms. As soon as they closed the door, Ms. Watson got down on her knees and pulled Ed's dick out.

As soon as Ed felt the warm sensation of her lips on his dick, he closed his eyes. He grabbed her head and started fucking her mouth. "Oh shit baby! Suck this dick! Damn," Ed said pumping in and out of her mouth. After a couple of minutes, Ed needed to feel her insides. He pulled her up and unbuckled her belt and pants. As he slid her pants down, he could see her tampon sticking out of her pussy. With no hesitation, Ed pulled it out and threw it in the trashcan.

He then pulled her shirt open exposing her breast. He started licking and palming them before putting one in his mouth and sucking on it. The whole time Ed was sucking Ms. Watson's titties, he had a finger in her pussy. It was so wet that Ed knew some of the wetness was her blood, but he didn't care and neither did she.

Ed bent over and took her pants all the way off. He then told her to lay on the floor. He got on top of her and she said, "Ed, I want you to fuck me now, please! I am so fucking horny!"

When Ed penetrated her walls, she dug her nails in his back and arched her back to meet his thrust. He started pumping faster and faster hitting her G-spot.

"Oh shit! Yessssss! Fuck me baby! Harder please! YESSSSSSSSS, RIGHT THERE," she said as she came all over Ed's dick.

Ms. Watson bit down on her lip to keep from screaming any louder. "This pussy feels so fucking good," Ed said, feeling himself about to bust.

After a couple of more pumps, he couldn't hold back any longer and he let his load off all inside of her.

"Damn that shit was good even after running the red light," Ed said fixing his clothes.

"You're a nasty mutha-fucker," Ms. Watson said smiling at him.

"You let me so I guess that makes two of us," Ed said looking out the door to see if anybody came in yet.

"Go back to your block while I clean up in here. It smells like sex and period juices all up in this bitch at the same time," she said looking for the air freshener in one of the drawers.

"Okay shorty, I'll see you tomorrow. I should be going home in a week or two so we definitely have to hook up then. Me, you, and Ms. McBride can get a room together," Ed said standing by the door.

"Oh shit, I can't wait baby. Just as long as the money is right. I'll even eat that bitch's asshole and yours too," Ms. Watson said seductively.

Ed shook his head and left the room to go back to his block.

* * *

It was Sunday night and everybody was sitting on the pod watching the Super Bowl. They had all made Chi Chi's and wraps and they even had sodas, chips, and cakes on the side. Ed had treated the whole pod so even the niggas that didn't have any money could eat. He figured since this would be his last week here that he should splurge a little.

They were watching Peyton Manning and the Broncos get beat down by the Seattle Seahawks when Tuck came over to Ed. "Yo, I got off the phone with my mom and she said shorty done ran off with my money," Tuck said angrily.

"I thought you said you were killing the blocks out there," Ed said meaning it as more of a question than a statement.

"I was, but ever since I've been in here and that dope has been on the rise, shit has slowed down. They said niggas ain't copping anything but black bags called *Numbers*," Tuck said.

"Numbers, huh? So that must be what EJ named his shit. He's coming up here tomorrow so I'll tell him to get you out," Ed said.

"Damn that's cool, but don't tell him that I can't pay him back. I still have to pay my connect his money. Looks like I'll be doing another hit for him like I did before," Tuck said not paying any attention to the way Ed looked at him.

"What hit did you do for him?" Ed asked tensing up.

"A couple of months ago when all of y'all first got popped, he sent me a kite telling me that his lawyer was going to send me a package. He told me to take care of the person that was in it and he would take care of me when he came home. When I received the information, I went and took care of it, leaving no witnesses," he said noticing a sudden change in Ed's demeanor.

"Where did this shit take place?" Ed asked

Tuck was a little skeptical at first, but he only did it to get them out so he told him. "In Southwest Philly over on 67th Street," he said not realizing that he had admitted to killing Ed's mom.

Ed stood up and walked away from the table without saying a word. He couldn't believe his childhood friend that he had went to war with and they both had slept over each other's cribs had deceived him like this. This was the ultimate deception. Ed caught an instant headache as he walked in his room and sat on his bunk.

He knew why his mom had been murdered, but he couldn't accept that it was EJ who had sent the hitman there. "All this time you knew who killed my mom and you acted like you didn't know," Ed said talking to himself.

"EJ, I'm going to get you for this when I get out of here, but I'm going to kill Tuck's bitch ass tonight," he said pulling his shank (homemade knife) out of the mattress.

Tuck was looking at Ed's cell when it finally hit him like a ton of bricks. "Oh shit! That was Ed's mom that I hit," he said to himself.

Without even thinking, Tuck ran over to the phone and called EJ. He had to let him know that he had slipped and admitted to Ed what had happened.

The phone rang three times before EJ answered. "You have a free call from, "Tuck," an inmate at a correctional facility…" before the operator could finish her speech, EJ pressed one and accepted the call.

"What up nigga! Why are you not a home yet?" EJ said as he was driving down 422 on his way home.

"Yo man, Ed knows. I'm sorry. We were talking and I mentioned it to him," Tuck said with nervousness in his voice.

EJ couldn't believe what he had just heard. Shit is about to get crazy now and he knew it. "Damn man; how the fuck did you let that hat out the bag? Never mind! We on the mutha-fucking phone. I'll have you out tonight. Just watch your back cause he's probably about to come at you," EJ said hanging up the phone. EJ knew this was going to come back and bite him in the ass. For every action, there's always a reaction and the repercussions for this would be death for someone.

Tuck hung up the phone and noticed that Ed was standing at his cell looking dead at him. He knew if he went over there that Ed would kill him. He already knew that Ed had his shank under his shirt.

Tuck decided to put himself in the hole until he got bailed out. He hoped that

EJ would have him out within the next few hours. Without wasting any time, Tuc stole on one of the niggas beside him on the phone with a two-piece putting him o his ass.

The C/O hit the button on his radio calling a code red. Ed started walking ove towards Tuck with this hand under his shirt. Before he could get close, six othe C/O's ran on the block tackling Tuck to the ground. Ed turned around and ran bac to his cell so he could hide his shank. "I'm going to get your bitch ass and that nigg EJ too when I get out," Ed said as tears formed in his eyes.

He immediately wiped them away making his heart turn cold. From tha moment on, Ed knew he wouldn't trust anyone else again. The streets would soo be feeling his pain and a lot of blood was going to be shed before it was all over.

That night, Ed wrote two letters. He sent one to Gene who he used to steal car with, telling him to form a team of killers because when he got home, they wer going to wet up the streets. The second letter was to his so-called best friend and h knew after this letter, there would be no turning back.

Dear EJ,

By now you know what this letter is about. How could you put a hit out on m mom without informing me first? So what, she was a rat. I thought we wer brothers. I might not have agreed with the decision, but we still should have talke about it. I know she was like a mother to you, but she was my blood so the decisio should have been mines to make, not yours.

Then on top of that, you had the audacity to try to cover it up so that I wouldn find out. See that's where you fucked up. Your hitman didn't leave any witnesses but you sure did. If you are going to play these street games, make sure you kno what you are getting yourself into. You have blood on your hands and pretty soo so will I. With that said, I'll be home in a week and I will be there to see you. Mak sure you come correct, cause I sure will.

~~Love~~ No More,
Ed

PS. Families are off limits. This is not about them. It's between me and you. I' going to kill you or die trying!

Ed finished the letter, cut his hand, and smeared blood all over it. After that, he folded it and placed it in an envelope. Ed knew once this went out that their bond was officially over. The two brothers were now at war and the only way for it to end would be death.

He walked over and placed the sealed letter in the mailbox. Ed walked away without any doubt in his mind that he was ready to kill.

CHAPTER 5

More Money Than You Can Count

E J was sitting on the couch reading the letter he had received yesterday to Loud Pack and Tuck. The girls were in the kitchen bagging up bundles and wrapping up logs of dope.

After he read the letter, he looked at his crew and said, "I guess we know what we have to do."

"How do you want to play this because this is going to get ugly before it gets better," Loud Pack asked.

"I guess it's time to put a group of killers together. That will be your job since you have ties all the way out to B-More. Have them all meet me at the new club that I rented on Broad and Girard. We will talk then. Right now, let's get back to this money because I have a lot of shit over there that needs to be in the streets," EJ said to Loud Pack as he pointed to all the dope on the tables.

"How do you want to distribute it to the blocks?" Loud Pack asked.

"Okay Tuck, I want you to drop off one hundred and ten logs over on 3rd and Harrison in Delaware to a dude name Dep. Tell him there's eleven hundred bundles in there and one hundred of them is his. Let him know that I want $20,000.00 back off of that. Then drop sixty logs off over in Rose Gate. That's on New Castle Avenue and someone by the name of Curt will be there. Tell him that it's six hundred bundles in there and he can keep one hundred for himself. He will owe me $10,000.00. Once you drop that off, then meet us at the club tonight around eleven," EJ said to Tuck as he went to the cabinet to grab the work he needed.

"Loud Pack, I think you need to take off now so that you can get back from Baltimore in time for the meeting. If you don't think that you will make it, hit me up before then. You already know what Trillz want, but now he wants ten. He said meet him at the same place in the Mondawmin Mall. He said call when you are in the city. Don't worry about the money. He will be paying as he goes along. He is our best customer so we have to keep him happy. So go on and get to it and I'll see you later," EJ said to Loud Pack.

EJ hit his out of town spots, but now he had to hit his Philly spots also. Just as he was about to dial her number, Tiff and Shannon walked in. They had been handling the Philly spots for him. They were also still in the fake ID and credit card business as well. EJ only made ten percent of their earnings because he wanted them to take over the business. "Hey sexy! What you calling me for? I'm right here," Tiff said giving EJ a hug.

"How you know I was calling your conceited ass?" EJ asked smiling as he gave Shannon a hug also.

"That's easy. You hung up as soon as you saw us walk in," Tiff said as she removed her coat and sat down on the couch.

EJ couldn't say anything. "You are too smart for your own good. Anyway, I'm glad that y'all made it. I need y'all to drop the work off at the spots out North and South Philly. I will take care of the West Philly spots since there is only two. You can give each spot fifty logs. Tell them I want $8,500.00 back off of them. I know they are going to probably cut it again because it's still pure, but I don't care as long as they have my money," EJ said to the girls.

"Do we need to collect anything while we are out there because we have some shit to do over in Jersey?" Shannon asked.

"You can keep the money with you and I'll get it later. Are y'all coming to the club tonight?" EJ asked.

"We wouldn't miss it for the world. Especially since it's the grand opening," Shannon with excitement in her voice.

They stayed and chilled with EJ for a while before leaving out to handle their business. EJ and the girls finished wrapping up the last of the logs in newspaper and then they stacked them away. He waited for them to get dressed so that he could drop them off on his way to make his drops.

In total, EJ had over a half a million dollars hitting the streets tonight and that was only what they owed him. That meant that it was going to be a lot of money in the streets thanks to him. He had the streets on smash and he had done it without Ed.

EJ, Jonay, Felicia, and Sharnell all jumped in Ed's Bentley. It was cold outside so the heat was comforting which allowed them to take their coats off or open them up once they got in the car.

"Are y'all going over to 48th Street or 42nd?" EJ asked Sharrell

"We are going home because we have to get ready to come to the club later tonight," Jonay said.

After EJ hit the two Southwest Philly spots and collected the money, he dropped Sharrell and Jonay off at home. Then he went to Lex Street and dropped off, before heading over to Mellon Street. His other drop was on Brown Street so he decided to go there after he left from Felicia's crib.

"So are you coming to the party tonight?" EJ asked Felicia as he stopped in front of her crib.

"If I get someone to watch my son I will. It's bad enough that I leave him with my mom all day while I'm working," she said as she put her coat back on.

EJ stared at her for a minute before saying, "Let me know if you can't make it and I'll stop pass to check up on you later."

"Alright, I will see you later and be careful out here," Felicia said before she closed the door and headed in her house.

When EJ pulled up on Brown Street, he saw the person he was looking for and beeped the horn at him. Once Mike seen who it was, he ran over and hopped in the car.

"What's up E? Did you bring that for me because the other shit is gone," Mike said getting warm.

"Yeah, that's why I'm here besides to collect that money from you," EJ said as he grabbed the bag out of the backseat.

"I got it coming right now," Mike said as he called his worker on the phone to bring him the money out of the stash house.

A couple of minutes later, a young boy walked out with a book bag and brought it over to the car. He passed it to Mike before running back into the house.

EJ took the bag and threw it into the backseat. "I'll see you in a week. If you need me before then, hit my cell."

"I sure will Cannon. Now let me get back to this dollar," Mike said giving EJ a pound before getting out of the car.

EJ headed back to Millick Street so he could count all the money that he had made for the week. He wanted to hurry up so that he could get a little rest before the grand opening of his new club tonight.

When he returned to the stash house, he grabbed the book bags and went in. He poured the money on the table, and his eyes got big at the sight of all the bills laying before him. It was too much money to count by himself. He had a money machine, but he still needed another body. EJ decided to call Erica and see where she was. He couldn't call Shannon, Tiff, Tuck, or Loud Pack cause they were all handling shit out of town. He didn't want to leave it there uncounted and he damn sure wasn't taking all of that dirty money home.

Erica answered her phone on the second ring. "Hello," she said.

EJ didn't know if she already knew what has happened or not so, he wanted to pick her brain first. "Hey baby girl, are you busy right now?" he asked her.

"No, I'm coming from 69th Street. Why? What's up?" she said.

"I need you to stop over on Millick Street to help me count this money. It's too much for one person to be counting," EJ said while watching Freestyle Friday on the 106 and Park show.

"Well you know I like money so what's the address and I'll come right now," Erica said while waiting for the light to change.

EJ gave her the address and ten minutes later, she was knocking at the door. He let her in and as soon as she saw all the money on the table, she rubbed her hands together in excitement.

"Damn boy! What bank you done robbed cause I know all that didn't come from that check shit," Erica said.

"Nawwww. Your boy is on to bigger and better shit now. I got those Number packets out in the street. I'm trying to lock the city down and every area around it," EJ said as he took her coat and laid it on the couch.

"Oh shit. Now you in the drug game too? Just be careful and don't trust anybody out there. You and my brother are the only two people I trust," Erica said.

Hearing that only made him feel even guiltier. Since Ed knew about the murder already, EJ decided that he might as well tell Erica before anybody else did. H didn't know how she would take it, but at that point, he didn't care about an consequences.

"Erica, I have to tell you something before we start counting that shit. This i important and I have to get it off my chest," EJ said while leading her over to th couch.

Once they were seated, EJ looked at Erica as she stared at him. "I wanted to tel you this before you heard it from someone else," EJ began.

Before he could even start, Erica interrupted him. "I know you put the contrac out on my mom. I talked to my brother the other day when I went to visit him. I'r going to tell you the same thing that I told him. The bitch shouldn't have never beer rocking with the pigs. She was lucky that I didn't find out first or I would be in jai right now," Erica said cold heartily.

EJ was shocked at what came out of her mouth. He thought that she would be trying to fight him or something right now. She acted as if it was nothing else to discuss. "Now are we going to count this money or not so I can go home," Eric said standing up.

EJ stood up and grabbed her arm. "But what about Ed? You know he's coming home in a couple of days and he wants to go to war. He's really mad at me abou that shit," he said.

"He told me that I wasn't his sister anymore because I felt like that. I tried to talk to him, but he ended the visit early and walked away. I don't want to see m brother or you get hurt so I hope that y'all will come to some kind of understanding and fix this feud. I know eventually he will come around because I'm his baby sister, but y'all have been friends forever. I just hope this beef will be squashed and y'all can continue to get money together," Erica said.

EJ didn't know what to say about that. He hoped that she was right, but just to be on the safe side, he already had Yahnise looking for a new and bigger house so they could move. He wasn't going to tell anybody about this place except for Nyi and Chris. He had already brought Chris in as his partner. One thing about him was he would shoot first and ask questions last. He grew up in the streets and stopped hanging in them once he opened his own car dealership. Since he had heard about the situation with Ed, he stepped out of his business attire and back into his stree shit. EJ knew he needed him so that's why he didn't try to stop him and made him his partner.

"Okay baby girl, let's get to this money," EJ said as they started counting all the money on the table.

* * *

At 9:00 p.m., EJ and Erica were finished counting the money. EJ had purchased two floor safes that would hold the money and two to hold the work. He had to get the basement door cut to get them down there. Altogether, he had four big ass safes down there. After they loaded all the money in the safes, EJ gave Erica $2,000.00 for helping him with the counting.

"Damn! Why you pay me this much money for only counting it?" she questioned.

EJ laughed and said, "I can take it back and give you less if you want."

"Shit, over my dead body," Erica said smirking.

"Well, I have to get dressed for the grand opening of my night club. Are you going to be there?" he asked her.

"I'll try to come. I have a date tonight, but we will come by there afterwards," Erica said giving EJ a kiss on his cheek before leaving.

EJ went outside and grabbed his clothes out of the car. He knew he didn't have enough time to drive all the way to Pottstown and back by eleven so he was going to get ready there.

After he called Yahnise and told her to meet him at the club, he went to take a shower. It was time to get ready for the grand opening of *Ziaire's*.

CHAPTER 6

The Ménage

When EJ arrived at Club Ziaire, the lines were going around the corner. There were so many people trying to get in that most of them wouldn't make it because the club would soon be filled to capacity. EJ stepped out of his Bentley GT wearing an all-black Prada suit with a pair of black Prada shoes. He had on a $50,000.00 watch that he got made from Johnny's Custom Jewelry. His watch had so much ice in it that if you turned the lights out, his watch could light up the whole room.

As soon as he walked up to the front door, the females, even the ones with their men, began wetting in their panties. They could smell money and they were counting dollar signs as they watched him enter the club.

After EJ greeted a few people, he headed upstairs to his office to get ready to meet with his team. EJ knew he had to make sure that he was prepared for anything that came his way. Now that he was in the game, people were going to try to take what he has worked so hard for.

When he got in his office, Tuck, Loud Pack, and these three niggas that EJ had never seen before were sitting there waiting for him. One of the men had long dreads and the other two had short cuts with waves. Loud Pack stood up and greeted EJ with a handshake. Then he introduced the men that came with him.

"This is Nice, Sheed, and Mel. Sheed and Mel are from the Wilson projects and

Nice is from 58th and Kingsessing. I grew up with these dudes and they are about that work. Anything you need done, they are the ones to see," Loud Pack said.

"Well it's a pleasure to meet all of you," EJ said shaking their hands.

He sat down at his desk before he started to explain why they were here. "A couple of months ago, a woman was murdered for being a snitch. That is the worst kind of human in the world besides pedophiles. I despise these two types of people and if it were up to me, they all would die a terrible death. Well anyway, the person that was killed, I ordered the hit. Her son and I were best friends. We grew up together and she was like a mother to me. He was my brother," EJ said making sure he had everyone's attention.

"After her death, he found out that I was the one who ordered the hit. Now he wants to go to war with me when he comes home from jail next week. I don't know what he has planned, but I want to be prepared. That is why y'all will be my security team. Y'all will be on my payroll starting now. So any damage that you cause that needs a cleanup crew, there is a number in these cell phones that I'm giving you under the name, cleaners. Just call it and everything will be taken care of," EJ said as he passed each man an iPhone.

"Those phones are business phones only so don't give the number out to anybody that is not on a business level. Any questions?" EJ asked.

No one responded so he continued. "Well, y'all can go and enjoy the party. Drinks are on the house tonight," EJ said as the men nodded their heads in approval. As they were heading for the door, Chris walked in.

"Hey, before you guys leave, I would like for you to meet your other boss and my partner, Chris. Chris this is Mel, Nice, and Sheed. You already know Loud Pack and Tuck," EJ said as they all shook Chris' hand.

"It was nice meeting y'all. Enjoy yourselves. There are a lot of fine women out tonight," Chris said as they left out.

When everybody was gone, Chris and EJ started talking about the new spots that he had added in Pottstown and the two he was going to get in Williamsport. As they were discussing business, EJ's cell rung. It was his wife so he answered right away. "Hey baby! Where are you?"

"We are pulling up now. Come out and meet us," Yahnise said as she pulled up to the front of the club in her new 2014 Mercedes Benz S class. EJ had purchased it from Chris' lot as soon as it came in.

"I'm on my way to the door now," EJ said heading down the stairs form his office and through the crowd to get his wife.

When he reached the door, he saw Yahnise stepping out of her Benz looking like a model followed by her sister Nyia. EJ knew she was going to be drinking so he got her a chauffeur to drive her around for the night.

Yahnise looked beautiful in a red Alexander McQueen pencil dress. Her beautiful red dress matched her black Christian Louboutin stilettoes with the red heels. She had her hair down, she had on a matching red diamond bracelet, and necklace set from Tiffany's that EJ had got her for her birthday. The whole set went with the red diamond ring on her finger. She was sparkling in more ways than one.

Nyia was also dressed to impress wearing an all-black Dolce & Gabbana strapless fitted dress that accented all of her curves. She had on some 5" metallic gold open toed Jimmy Choo shoes that had straps that went up to her mid-calf. She wore a white diamond bracelet and necklace set. also from Tiffany's.

EJ and Chris stood side by side, as their ladies approached them like they were the life of the party. "Hey beautiful, I'm glad you could make it," EJ said giving Yahnise a passionate kiss in front of all the gawking onlookers. Chris did the same as they grabbed their men arms and headed inside.

Drinks stopped being free for everybody at 11:00 except EJ's crew. It was now 12:30 a.m. and the club was in full get-money mode. The club had two floors with different music playing on each. Both floors also had a counter where you could purchase either soul or seafood. EJ had hired a couple of chefs fresh out of college and they were worth every penny he spent on their paychecks.

EJ, Yahnise, Chris, and Nyia were sitting up in V.I.P. drinking and having a good time. EJ was drinking his famous cranberry and orange juice while everyone else was sipping on some Ace of Spades and Mo'scoot (for the women).

"This shit is jumping up in here. My brother-in-law got this building packed," Nyia said feeling tipsy.

"I couldn't have done it without y'all support though; especially without my beautiful wife," EJ said leaning over and kissing Yahnise on the cheek.

"Ummmm, don't start nothing you can't finish, big boy," Yahnise said seductively.

Everyone burst out laughing and started bobbing their heads to the music. "So baby, I want you to get used to this place because this will be you and Nyia's club to run," EJ said looking at the ladies.

They both hugged EJ all excited about their new club. They knew they could handle it because they had both gone to school for business management, plus EJ had hired a more experienced manager to help them. The lady had over twenty years of experience and she was also the one who got the liquor license for him.

At 2:00 a.m., the club was closing and everybody began clearing out. EJ walked his wife and Nyia to the car while Chris started counting the money with Loud Pack and Tuck.

"I'll be home in the morning so we can have some family time," EJ said to Yahnise as he kissed her.

"Make sure you do because I need this pussy beat up on because you been neglecting your responsibilities lately," she said.

"I know baby and I will take care of that and so much more as soon as I get home," he said while grabbing her ass and squeezing it.

After the driver pulled off, EJ's phone started ringing. "Hello," he said answering it.

"Are you busy right now?" Jonay questioned.

"No, what's up? Ain't you in the club right now?" EJ said.

"I was, but me and Felicia are on our way to the Hilton. We need you to stop by so we can give you something," she said.

"Why didn't y'all leave it here before you left? I might not be able to make it there because we have a lot of money to count from tonight's proceeds," EJ said.

"You have to come and it won't take that long. You'll be back before you know it. This really is important and I don't think you want to leave this with us," she said sounding tipsy.

EJ sighed and looked at his watch. "I'll be there in a half hour. What's the room number?" he asked.

"Room 1022 and hurry up," Jonay said before hanging up.

EJ went back in to tell Chris that he was about to roll out. He wanted to go see what was so important.

* * *

EJ pulled up to the Hilton and headed up to the room that Jonay said they were in. When he knocked on the door, Felicia answered it wearing a robe. She looked like she had just got out of the shower. "Come in and have a seat. I'll be right back," she said disappearing into the bathroom.

EJ went over and took a seat on the chair near the window. "Hurry up because don't have all day and what is it that I don't want to leave without taking?" EJ sai staring at the bathroom.

Felicia and Jonay both walked out the bathroom naked. "These wet, horn pussies," they both said in unison.

EJ's whole demeanor changed at the sight of the two beautiful women as the walked over to the bed and began kissing each other. He started getting comfortabl as he took off his coat to enjoy the show.

Felicia began playing with Jonay's pussy while they continued kissin passionately. EJ didn't know why he was still there because he didn't want to mi business with pleasure, but as he watched the two girls get it on, on the king-size bed; his little head (dick) prevailed in the thinking process.

The girls were now getting real freaky as they started eating each other's pussy EJ walked over to the bed and stuck two fingers in Felicia's pussy. The excitemen of Jonay's tongue and EJ's fingers caused her to cum quickly. "Ohhhh shit Yesssss! I'm cummmming... Ohhhhh right there baby," Felicia said squirting al over Jonay's mouth and on EJ's fingers.

Jonay sat up and crawled to the front of the bed where EJ was standing. Sh unzipped his pants and pulled his dick out. She took him into her mouth causing E to moan a little from the warm sensation. While Jonay was giving EJ head (suckin his dick), Felicia got off the bed and came up in the back of him helping him tak off his clothes.

After his clothes were off, all three of them got on the bed. EJ laid down on hi back as Felicia started sucking his dick. He grabbed Jonay, positioned her pussy o his face, and began eating her pussy.

"FUUUUUCK! YESSSSSS! Eat this pussy baby! Right there! That's my spot!' Jonay screamed as EJ fingered her, sucked, and licked on her clit.

Felicia got up and sat on EJ's dick. She started riding him while she playe with Jonay's titties. Jonay leaned back into Felicia and started grinding her pussy o EJ's mouth. "I'm about to cum! Keep doing that shit with your tongue!" sh screamed as she came in EJ's mouth.

EJ felt himself about to cum so he pulled Felicia off of him. "Get on your knee and put that ass in the air," he said to Jonay.

She quickly did what she was told anticipating the pleasure that was yet to come. As EJ slid inside of her walls from behind, Felicia laid down in front of Jonay with her legs in the air as Jonay buried her face in Felicia's pussy again.

Jonay was throwing her ass back trying to match every pump that EJ was giving her. "Oh shit! You are hitting my spot! YESSSSSSS! RIGHT THERE!" she screamed out in ecstasy.

EJ wasn't done with her yet. Her pussy was way wetter than Felicia's so he knew she was a squirter. He had to make sure though, so he turned her over on her back and pushed her legs all the way up to her shoulders. He entered her and started fucking her so hard that tears came to her eyes. "Take this dick bitch! You wanted it so bad, well here it is," he said as he continued to pound away.

Felicia was laying there fingering herself the whole time while watching as EJ was fucking the shit out of Jonay. He motioned for her to come over there and without hesitation; he lifted her up on his shoulders and buried his tongue inside of her pussy while still fucking Jonay.

"Oh shit! Eat this pussy, baby. I'M ABOUT TO CUM AGAIN!" Felicia screamed. EJ was about to cum also.

Jonay kept pumping and grabbing EJ's legs trying to get the full thrust as she came for the second time all over his dick. He wanted to get his shit off now so he put Felicia down, bent her over on the bed, and began drilling her pussy from the back.

She was hollering, "YEEESSSSSS EJ! I'M CUMING!" She bust and now it was his turn. EJ pulled out in time to bust all over her ass. Jonay started licking the cum off of Felicia's ass. Felecia turned around and sucked all of the cum off of his dick trying to get his shit back up for another round.

"I can't do this anymore. My wife is home waiting for me," he said as he got up and headed for the bathroom.

While he was in the shower, the girls came and got in with him. They ended up getting their round two after all. EJ didn't end up getting home until 10:00 that morning and he was greeted by his angry wife. He lied to her and said they had to count all the money over again amongst other things. She believed him, but she knew that it was more to it than that. She just hoped that he wasn't out there cheating on her.

CHAPTER 7

Home Sweet Home

Ed was finally home because Jersey had failed to extradite him to face his gun charges. He was a free man now with murder on his mind. He was sitting in Gene's house with six other niggas talking about what they planned to do.

"I see that nigga really got the city on lock with that Numbers shit, huh?" Ed asked Gene as he sipped on some Hennessey.

"Yeah and it's hard to sell our shit because of that. I mean, our pills and loud are still killing the streets, but the crack is not. Even the niggas that are selling the shit in weight won't let us cop because we fuck with you," Gene said.

"Well if they won't let us cop from them, then it's time to go rob and take what we want then," Ed said as he cocked his hammer (gun) back.

Ed always had a thing for 40 caliber guns. He felt as though they were more reliable than any other gun he had ever used. He was the one who turned EJ on to them. Just thinking about that shit made his temperature rise. He wanted to kill him in the worst way and he was going to get his chance sooner or later.

"Alright, let's load up and go see who we can hit," Gene said to his men. Then he looked at Ed and said, "Are you ready for this because it's no turning back once we get started?"

"I was born ready," is all Ed said as they headed out the door to the two stolen cars that awaited them.

* * *

It was still daylight out when Ed and his crew got to West Philly. They were camping out on Brown Street watching the abundance of traffic that was going in and out of the house. There was a young boy that would stand on the porch and collect the money before sending the junkies in to get their fix. From the looks of everything, they were running a smooth operation.

Ed was paying attention to the area around him because he didn't want to slip up as he did when he ran up on a block before and they had shooters on the roof. He watched the second floor windows looking for any signs of danger. When he saw that no one was watching, he changed his mind about them running a smooth operation.

"Look, they don't even have shooters on the roof or in the second floor windows. This is going to be an easy lick (robbery). Okay young boy, you know what to do," Ed said to the dude in the backseat. The guy nodded his head and stepped out the car. The passengers in the second car hopped out too once they saw the guy step out of the first car. Ed and Gene were waiting for the shit to go down before they were going to jump out.

The dude from the backseat walked up to the porch and waited to be called in. The dealer was taking the money from the man in front of him and once he received his money, he sent him in. Then he looked at his next customer. "Yo, what do you need?" he asked as the man from the backseat stepped up on the steps.

"Let me get two bundles," he said passing the boy the money.

As soon as he stuck his hand out, the dude grabbed both of his hands and pulled him down the steps towards him.

One of the other goons pulled out his gun that was hidden in his jacket and aimed it at the dealer. "Don't more or say a word and you will get to live to see another day," he said pushing the guy into the alleyway next to the house.

The other fiends in line didn't know what had happened and they really didn't care. All they were concerned with was getting in the house.

Ed and Gene were already out the car when they saw the first move. Gene walked up to the boy who was being held in the alleyway who couldn't have been any older than sixteen. "How many people are in the house?" he asked pointing a gun at the boy's face.

The boy was scared, but he played the brave roll and little did he know; that was his first mistake. He spit in Gene's face and as soon as the spit hit him, Gene began pistol-whipping him. Once the boy had a bloody face and was unconscious, Ed pulled him off of him.

"Let's do this the hard way then," Ed said as he signaled for the crew to get ready to run up in the house.

Ed counted to three and all eight of the men ran in with their weapons aimed to kill. "DON'T NOBODY MOVE!" Ed yelled as he and all of the men pointed their guns at the fiends and the workers.

"Lay down! You know what the fuck this is," Gene said as he nodded to two of his men to go check upstairs while the others went to check the basement.

"We want all the money and work and we'll leave here without anybody dying," Ed said pointed his gun all around.

Gene led one of the workers to the other room to show him where the money and work was located. When he came back out with a trash bag half-full, Ed smiled. A few seconds later, another dude came from the basement with a book bag and Ed smiled and said," Let's get the fuck out of here!"

They all started leaving. Ed and Gene left out first with the money and work while the last two men backpedaled out the door behind them making sure nobody moved.

As soon as they made it out the door, one of the workers jumped to his feet and lifted the pillow on the couch grabbing his Riot Pump hidden there. "Fuck all that! I'm not going out like that!" he said cocking it and heading for the door.

When he made it outside, he saw the men jumping in their cars. He started firing not even thinking or caring about anyone's safety.

BOOM!

BOOM!

BOOM!

BOOM!

Gunfire was all that was heard as he fired shot after shot after the robbers.

He never noticed that one of the fiends had crept outside also, but the fiend had a gun in her hands. She walked behind the dealer and put two shots in his head.

POP!

POP!

The shots killed him before he even hit the ground. Then the woman took off running down the street to a car that was waiting for her.

She jumped in, left the crime scene while all the other junkies ran out the house, and scattered everywhere.

Ed and Gene smiled as they looked at all the dope and money that they had got from the robbery. "One down and plenty more to go. We gonna make his life a living hell before I bring him to his knees and kill him," Ed said looking out the window as they drove down Lancaster Avenue to their next destination.

* * *

They were now sitting back at Gene's house counting the money and dope that they had just robbed for Ed. Altogether, they had hit three of his spots and killed all of the workers at the lost spot that they had hit.

"Them niggas went out swinging at the last house. Don't they know who they were going up against," Ed said smoking some loud.

"Who was the bitch that showed up at all the spots making sure no one ambushed us as we were leaving? She's a real gangsta bitch. I like the way she was laying those niggas down," one of the dudes said.

"Don't worry. All of you will get to meet her soon. Let's get back to this money first," Ed said thinking about his down ass bitch who had been putting in that work.

After they finished counting everything, they had taken $15,000.00 in cash and $12,000.00 in dope. "So what do you want to do with this dope? We can't sell it with his stickers still on it," Gene said looking at the dope.

"Well we just have to change the name and then put it in one of our spots out North. Once we hit some more of his cribs, he just might come out of hiding and go head up with me," Ed said.

"Well let's change the bags from black to red and then stamp them with the name, "Blood Game." That is how we got it, and we're not afraid to make it rain in the streets with blood," Gene said.

Ed thought about it for a minute and then he agreed with Gene. "That's not a bad idea. You take care of that while I go see one of my jump-offs. My wife got hers for the last couple of days and now it's time to share some of this good stuff with some of my other girls," Ed said as he went over to the table with the money on it. "I'm going to take ten g's of the money. You keep the other five and split the dope with the workers. Tell them what they make, they can have. Once we hit the big houses, the money will get better."

Ed gave Gene a pound and left to go see a longtime friend of his. He hoped he got the welcome that he was looking for, but if not, then oh well.

* * *

Ed headed over to a girl's house in Southwest Philly by the name of Theresa. She had been with him during his whole bid by coming up to see him whenever his wife didn't. He wanted to say thanks by giving her a token of his appreciation.

When he pulled up to her crib, she was heading out the door with two other women. He beeped the horn on is Dodge Charger and when she saw who was beeping at her, she stopped and smiled. Ed rolled down the window. "What's up Ma? Where are you headed at 9:30 at night?" he asked her.

"I'm about to go skating with a couple of my friends out in Franklinville," she said leaning into the car window.

Ed looked at her wearing those sexy tights and immediately wanted to fuck her. "I'm trying to see you right now. Can you cancel for me?"

"Why don't you come with us, and afterwards we will give you our thanks," she said looking at her two girlfriends standing beside her.

Ed took one glance at the two girls and his dick instantly got hard. He wanted all three of them. He knew about Franklinville. They let you smoke and drink there so he said what the hell. "Okay. We'll take my car. Tell your friends to come on," he said hitting the locks on the doors.

As they started to get in the car, Ed noticed how thick they all were. The two friends were both wearing sweatpants and it looked like their asses were shaking from the front. Ed couldn't wait to fuck all three of them. Life was going to feel even better later on. He made a mental note to check his overseas account later to make sure Ed hadn't tried any bullshit. He was going to change the pin numbers and access codes on his accounts.

They all jumped in, and Ed headed for Jersey. "Hey ladies. What's good?" Ed said as he put on a DVD for the ladies to watch while he drove.

One of the ladies said, "You is what's good when we get back. I hope you can handle all this ass." As if on cue, all three of the ladies started laughing.

"Shit, you keep talking like that, I'll turn this mutha-fucka around, and we can find out if I can handle it," Ed said smirking.

"You'll get your chance, big man," Theresa said as they all enjoyed the bootlegged DVD of "Ride Along" with Kevin Hart.

Whey they pulled up to Franklinville, the place was jumping. They couldn't even find a parking spot because it was so packed. Ed parked near the curve at the entrance.

They all hopped out and went into the skating rink. After Ed paid for everybody, he headed over to the section where he could blow (smoke) while the girls put on their skates and headed to the floor to skate.

As Ed was in the smoking and drinking section, he never noticed the nigga that was watching him and talking on his phone.

"Yeah the nigga came up in here about ten minutes ago with some bitches. What do you want me to do?" the young boy asked.

He was at one of the houses that Ed had robbed earlier. By them coming in with no mask on, he easily recognized him.

"Wait for him to come out and handle that. If anybody gets in the way, take care of them too," Chris said. He wanted to call EJ and see what he wanted to do, but he was busy trying to make up with his wife. He felt as though he was making the right call, so fuck it.

"That's all I need to hear. I'll handle that nigga when we get on the highway," the young boy said.

The young boy hung up and let his man that had come with him know what was going on. They enjoyed the rest of the night, but they also kept an eye on their prey.

* * *

It was midnight and everybody was heading for their respective cars. The two young boys watched as Ed and the three girls jumped in their car and pulled off. They pulled off right behind them. It was easy to follow them because they were all heading in the same direction.

Ed was high as hell and he was really feeling himself. He told one of the girls to drive while he was in the backseat getting head from Theresa. "Damn girl! Look at you taking all that dick in your mouth. Can I taste it too?" Jazz said.

"It's plenty of room back here. Come on," Ed said as he watched Jazz climb in the backseat. They were so occupied with their sexual favors, that they never even noticed the two thugs preparing to spray their car.

"As soon as we get off of fifty-five, it's on so stay with them," the passenger said. They didn't know who was driving because the windows on the car was tinted and it was very dark on route fifty-five.

Ed had Theresa and Jazz's pants off and he was playing with Jazz's pussy while Theresa was sucking his dick. Meka was mad because she had to drive. She wanted in on the action, but she had to wait until they got home.

"When we get home, you owe me a round by myself before you give them some more," she said sucking her teeth.

"I got you, baby girl," Ed said as he moved Theresa's head. He wanted to fuck Jazz skinny ass so bad. She was real skinny with a fat ass. He had to get some of that before they got home. "Get on top of this dick girl," he said as he pushed the front seat up.

Jazz sat on his dick with her back leaning on his chest. She started riding his dick while Theresa was fingering her clit.

"Oh shit! Your dick is too big! You are killing this pussy! Ohhhhh shit! Baby damn!" she moaned as Ed dicked her down.

They were so deep in their action that they didn't see the car on the side of them with the window down and the gun pointed out of it until it was too late.

POP!

POP!

POP!

POP!

POP!

Gunfire was all that was heard as the windows to Ed's car shattered all over them.

"What the fuck?" Ed said as he pushed Jazz off of him grabbing his forty caliber off the floor.

He began letting off shots while the girls were screaming.

BLOCA!

BLOCA!

BLOCA!

BLOCA!

The car that was shooting at them all of a sudden swerved and hit the side rail before flipping over five times.

Meka was a true gangsta. She didn't panic when the windows shattering. She started driving faster while trying to duck the shots.

"Is everybody good?" Ed asked the girls.

Everybody answered except for Theresa. When Ed looked over at her, she was leaning against the door with blood coming out the side of her head. "OH NO! NOT THERESA! PLEASE, NO, NO, NO! GET UP THERESA!" Jazz said hysterically while crying.

Ed was silent because he knew she was already gone. Ed knew they had to quickly get out of this bullet-riddled car. He hoped that they could get past the tollbooth without getting pulled over.

Once they made it pass the tollbooth, he told Meka where to go so that he could ditch his car and get another one. He didn't know who took aim at him, but he had a strange feeling that it was his old friend. Little did he know, but he had just upped the ante and he was going to get back at him real soon. For now, he had to dispose of this body that was in his car and get himself cleaned up.

The girls were in the streets so they knew what it was. He didn't have any problem convincing them about what had to be done. They were really upset that their best friend was dead. They didn't even know how they were going to explain this to her two-year-old son. How do you tell a two year old that their mommy will never be coming home again? They promised to take care of him though, and Ed was going to make sure that all of them were good.

He was thinking the whole time, "How did I get caught slipping again?" He was caught with his pants down for real this time. He laughed to himself from that thought.

CHAPTER 8

Back On the Job

Detective Harris didn't get the promotion he was looking for. He was lucky that he didn't get a demotion for the bullshit that he had done. Now he was at his desk working on a murder case that happened on Brown Street a couple of days ago. The Commissioner took him out of the Fraud Division and he had put him in homicide. Detective Harris didn't mind the transfer because now he got to work with his friend Kathy Myers from the Crime Scene Investigation (CSI) Unit.

He was thinking about all the shit that had happened over the last few months and how he had lost that case like that. That whole thing had left a sour taste in his mouth. He knew he was wrong, but he still couldn't accept the fact that they tried to make a mockery out of him and his team. He figured that he might as well get rich off of them.

Detective Harris had been hearing about a new drug that was terrorizing the streets called Numbers. So far, he hadn't run across it, but he knew it was only a matter of time before he did. What bothered him the most was, how it all of a sudden came into existence after Edward and Eric both had come home. Really Eric because Edward was still incarcerated when it hit the streets. Detective Harris had decided to extort them. He was becoming more and more of a bad cop since he couldn't get his promotion.

He had decided to hit the streets and pay Edward and Eric a little visit. He had to track that Numbers drugs down and it would lead him right to them. He left his office smiling at the possibility of making a lot of money off of the two scums.

* * *

EJ had just left club Ziaire's and he was heading to his stash house. He and his wife were trying to reconcile their differences. Lately she had been suspicious of him cheating when he came in real late so he had been coming home early every night since. He thought that would lighten her suspicions a little. They had got finished having lunch together, so he left her to finish her preparations for Friday. She had booked Meek Millz to perform at the club, so she had a lot of paperwork to prepare and sign.

As he was heading through Fairmont Park near Parkside Avenue, he noticed the Ford Taurus behind him. He didn't think anything of it until the occupant turned his flashers and sirens on, signaling for him to pull over.

"What the fuck do this piece of shit want now?" EJ questioned pulling over noticing that it was the detective that had tried to set him up.

Detective Harris stepped out of his vehicle and approached EJ's car. He had his hand on his gun just in case EJ tried something. When Detective Harris saw that EJ was the only one in the car, he asked him to step out of the car.

EJ reluctantly did as he was asked. "Why are you fucking with me now? Don't you have some evidence to plant on somebody else," EJ said smirking at the detective.

"I would first like to apologize for that, and I assure you that it won't happen again. I'm here to make a proposal to you if you are interested," Detective Harris said.

EJ didn't trust him one bit. He knew the detective had something up his sleeve, but he wasn't sure what it was. He decided to play his little game to see where it was going. "I'm listening, but I don't have all day so start talking," EJ said leaning on his car.

"Well as you can see, I came in peace. I know that you are the one behind this new drug on the streets. I've been watching you ever since you came home," Detective Harris lied trying to see EJ's reaction.

Once he had seen that he had his attention, he continued. "I can keep the heat off of you and let you eat if you bring me in. You pay me once a month and whenever something comes across my desk, I will let you know. If any competition gets in the way, I'll help you eliminate them," he said waiting for a response.

EJ thought about this for a minute. He knew that it would be good to have a dirty cop on his team. He would just have to keep an eye on him. "So how much will this little arrangement cost me?" EJ questioned.

"How's twenty grand a month? That will include all access to my department's resources," he said.

EJ couldn't help but to think of all the shit that he could do with the law on his side so he agreed to Detective Harris demands. "I hope that this is not another one of your scams," EJ said shaking hands with the Detective.

"As long as the money is coming in, we will never have a problem mutha fucka," Detective Harris said to himself, as he got back in his car and left.

* * *

After Detective Harris left EJ, he went to see what he could dish out of the other person. He had found out that EJ and Ed were no longer working together so he figured he would try to get paid from the both of them. He knew that both of them had a lot of money and he had his hands on both of their collars.

Detective Harris pulled up to a gas station on Island Avenue, and waited patiently for the person to pull up that he was waiting on. After five minutes, Ed pulled in the gas station and parked next to Detective Harris' car. Ed got out, went over to the Detective's car, and got in.

Detective Harris knew that Ed was pumping red baggies called "Blood Game" out of the Karmen Suites Apartment complex. He had arrested one of his worker and promised to let him go if he told Ed that he wanted to have a meeting with him.

"Nice of you to make it on such a short notice. I thought you didn't get my message," Detective Harris said.

"So what is this all about? I don't like dealing with the pigs and you are a pig. The only thing coming out of this meeting is me having to pay you to have free reign over the streets. My question to you is, how much and what's in it for me?" Ed said getting straight to the point.

"I see you are not as naive as Eric. So to answer your question, twenty grand a month and you will have all access to law enforcement resources. You'll be the first to know about any raids or indictments, and if you have any problems with the competition, I'll take care of it," Detective Harris said.

"First off, don't ever mention that niggas name in the same sentence as mine again. I don't want anything to do with him or you if you are making the same proposal to the both of us," Ed said mean mugging Detective Harris.

He looked at Ed and he was about to say something, but he shook his head and let him continue.

"Secondly, if we are going to do business, you will do as I say and not the other way around. I also would like you to take care of someone to let me know that you are on my team and no one else's," Ed said looking at the detective.

Detective Harris thought about it for a minute. *"I can easily trick both of these niggas to paying me every month. They wouldn't even know it because they are beefing with each other so it's on and I will be forty grand richer every month,"* Detective Harris said to himself. Then he looked over to Ed and said, "Edward we have a deal and just name the person."

Ed looked at the Detective and smiled. "The name is Tuck, and I knew you would see things my way," Ed said getting out of the car.

"For now my man, just for now," Detective Harris thought as he pulled off to head home for the night.

* * *

It was Friday night and the club was letting out so the cops were deep outside. Detective Harris was waiting on the person he was looking for. He wasn't worried about being noticed because of all the other uniformed and plain-clothes officers that was out there. Meek Millz had killed the stage tonight with some of his old and new music. Detective Harris didn't so he didn't bother with going in the club. He had been sitting outside all night until it was over. Seeing all the cars and people, he knew the club had to have made well over two hundred grand tonight.

After about another thirty minutes of waiting, the person that Detective Harris was waiting for came out of the club with his girl and headed for his parked car in front of the club. As soon as they pulled off, Detective Harris pulled up behind him.

He followed them until they got to the College Circle on 25th and Girard. He then hit his lights for them to pull over.

As soon as he made sure no one was outside, he pulled the gun out of his glove compartment and placed a silencer on it. Then he tucked it in his jacket as he got out and walked up to the driver's window.

The driver rolled the window down and waited for Detective Harris to get close.

"What the fuck do you want man? Business hours are over until tomorrow. I'm not paying you to be harassing me every time you see me. Now get the fuck out of my face and go find someone else to bother," the driver said while his girl laughed at him clowning the cop.

Detective Harris looked at them and said, "You are right, you are not paying me at all, you little shit." He pulled out the gun and aimed it at the driver who instantly stopped laughing along with the girl in the passenger seat.

"Wait! What are you doing?" the driver asked.

"Just business, nothing personal. I didn't know you had something to do with Ed's mom being killed. You also killed my star witness so this is for both of us," Detective Harris said right before he squeezed the trigger.

PHHH!

PHHH!

PHHH!

Was all that was heard as the driver's body and head took two bullets a piece. The woman in the passenger seat was screaming so loud that he thought someone would hear her.

PHHH!

PHHH!

PHHH!

He hit her with two shots to the heart and one through the head silencing her for life.

Then he ran back to his car and pulled off leaving the two bodies to be found by some random person walking by. He did what Ed had asked, now it was time to get this money.

As Detective Harris headed home, he hoped what he had just did wasn't a setup on Ed's part because if it was, he wasn't going to have a problem rocking him to sleep also. He wished he had thought about that before he had done it, but the damage had already been done. He just hoped that this wouldn't come back and bite him in the ass.

He stopped and picked himself up a couple of beers before heading home to his wife. Tomorrow he was going to call his old partner and see if he was interested in getting in on the action. First, he would have to see where his head was. There was no room for mistakes, he needed someone on his team that he could trust with his life, and he was the only person who fit that criteria.

Detective Harris knew he was playing a deadly game with the two ex-friends, he just hoped that he didn't get caught.

CHAPTER 9

Deception

EJ was sitting in his bedroom playing poker online when he heard Yahnise come in the house. She ran up the stairs all excited and came in the room yelling, "Guess who is here from California?" she asked while leaning over giving him a passionate kiss.

He knew only one person in her life could make her that happy to see them. "Let me guess, Sonja," EJ said.

"Yes baby! My best friend is back. I saw her when I was at the mall and she just got back with no place to stay right now. I told her that she could stay with us until she finds a crib. It will only be for about a month. Is that okay with you?" Yahnise said as she started rubbing EJ's dick through his shorts.

She knew how to get what she wanted from him. "You're always cheating," EJ said as he pulled her on his lap and started squeezing her titties.

Although EJ remembered Sonja to be a gold digging bitch, he knew it had been a while since his wife had seen her. The last time Yahnise had seen Sonja was right after their graduation. They always talked on the phone, but that was it. "Whatever you want, baby. Show her the rooms and see which one she wants," he said as he continued to play with her titties.

"Thank you baby. I got you later, on what you really want. Right now we are about to do some catching up. Come on down and say hello," she said getting up and pulling him up off the bed.

"Give me a few minutes. I can't come down like this," EJ said pointing to his dick sticking out of his shorts.

Yahnise laughed and went back downstairs with her friend. EJ finished his game of poker and he was about to go downstairs when Ziaire came into the room.

"Daddy, daddy, can we go outside and play?" he asked running fast with his little legs.

Ziaire was two and a half years old and if one didn't know any better, he looked like he was ten by the way he talked.

EJ loved him to death. "Come on little man, let's go see mommy's friend first and then we will go outside," EJ said lifting him up and carrying him downstairs.

When he came down the stairs, he heard the women in the living room talking. EJ walked in and saw Sonja sitting on the couch. She looked even more beautiful than she did in high school. She favored the singer Mya. Her ass was so round that it looked like she had implants. Her hair was long and it came damn near down to her lower back. EJ had to admit that she really looked good.

"Hey Sonja, how are you doing?" EJ said as he put Ziaire down and gave him a hug.

"Look at the boss all grown up. Yeah, your wife told me all about you," she said hugging EJ and holding on to him a little bit too long.

EJ stepped back and noticed that she was checking him out. He knew he would have to watch out for her while she was here.

"Well let me go outside before little man gets mad. I'll see y'all when I get back in. Do you want me to carry your stuff upstairs for you?" EJ asked politely.

"Thank you EJ. I picked the room right across from the bathroom," Sonja said.

EJ was wondering why she picked the room next to theirs, but he brushed it off as a coincidence. He ran the two suitcases upstairs to the room and then he went outside with his son to play in the yard.

* * *

Yahnise and Sonja left and went to Limerik Outlets to do some shopping. They spent over ten thousand dollars on crazy stuff. They were just happy to be together once again and they were enjoying each other's company like they used to do when they were in high school. They were sitting at a table eating and catching up with one another.

"So, how was it in Cali? Did you meet any rich people while you were out there? I know how your ass is," Yahnise said while eating some fries.

"Girl, I was messing with some rapper out there and he treated me good until I went to see him at work one day and some ugly bitch was sucking his little dick in the studio. I tried to pull that bitch's weave out, but his security threw me out instead. They didn't even throw out the other woman. Come to find out, it was his baby's mother and new artist. Girl, I was pissed when they told me that. Other than that, I met and chilled with a couple of other guys, but nothing serious," Sonja said.

"What made you come back home, and why were you out here at King of Prussia?" Yahnise asked.

"Actually that's where the Grey Hound had stopped. I didn't want to sit on the bus so I started walking around the mall. That's when I saw you. To tell the truth, I really didn't know where I was going. I was going to get a hotel room at the Hilton or somewhere like that until I found a place," Sonja said taking a sip of her drink.

"Well you can stay with us as long as you want to. Our home is your house because you are my sister," Yahnise said smiling.

"Thanks girl and I really do appreciate it. I'm supposed to go look at some houses and apartments next week. Anyway, enough about me, I see you and EJ are doing well. You finally found someone to take that kitty, huh?"

"Man, he can't get enough of this, and I can't get enough of that good dick, girl!" Yahnise said looking like she had just had an orgasm.

"It ain't that good, is it?" Sonja said remembering how big his dick looked in the ball shorts he was wearing earlier.

"I'll tell you all about it on our way home. It's getting late and I know my boys are hungry. Let's get out of here and pick them up a pizza," Yahnise said as they left the mall with what seemed like one hundred bags.

* * *

The time was 11:00 p.m. and EJ had finished checking his bank accounts online. Savino had washed over $500,000.00 for him in the last month. All his accounts were looking really good. He had to go meet his connect in the morning so he stayed home tonight with his family. Chris was running the dope business and Nyia had the club tonight because Yahnise was off.

He went and laid on the bed while Yahnise was in the shower. Ziaire and Sonja were in their rooms, probably sleeping. Sonja had been real good with Ziaire. He had been playing with her all night ever since they came back from the mall.

Yahnise came out of the bathroom, dripping wet with a towel wrapped around her. EJ watched her as she started putting Victoria's Secret lotion on. His dick got hard at the sight of his wife's naked body.

He grabbed her while she was bent over, rubbing his dick on her ass. She leaned back grinding on his dick. He turned her around and lifted her onto the bed spreading her legs open wide. He began to kiss up her inner thighs until he reached her freshly shaved pussy.

He stuck his tongue out and massaged her clit, making her scream out in pure delight. "OHHHH SHIT BABY! RIIIGGGGGGT THERE! OH IT FEELS SO GOOD!" she yelled as she grabbed his head and grinded her pussy on his tongue.

That didn't know that Sonja was still up and could hear them in the next room. They also forgot that they had left their door cracked. All the stories that Yahnise had told her on the way home had her curious, so when she heard them, she decided to go peek through the keyhole.

When she came out of her room and saw their door cracked, she got excited because she would have a better view. When she peeked in, all she saw was Yahnise's legs in the air and EJ's head between them eating her pussy. Sonja's pussy began to pulsate from the scene she was watching. She had on a pair of boy shorts and a wife beater with no bra. She began touching herself as she watched the two.

EJ's tongue was circling Yahnise clitoris driving her insane. "Ahhhh, damn baby! I'm about to cum! Pleaseeeee don't make me cum yet! I want to feel you inside of me, right now! Ahhhhhh, I'm cumming! DAMN!" Yahnise said as EJ drank all of her juices.

He wasn't done yet, though. He started kissing every part of her body as he slowly moved up to her breast and teased her nipples. She was in pure excitement as EJ slid inside of her. She closed her eyes and relished the fullness of his dick in her soaking wet pussy. "FASTER BABY; FASTER!" she screamed as EJ fucked her harder and faster.

Sonja was at the door looking with two fingers in her pussy wishing that it were her in there with EJ. She started fingering herself faster and faster with every pump, that EJ gave his wife. "Ummmmm shit," she said opening her eyes to make sure they didn't hear her.

"Oh fuck yes! God, give it to me baby! Yesssssss! I'm about to cum again!" Yahnise said as EJ stopped and turned her over entering her from behind.

"Tell me how you want it," EJ said as he started drilling her from behind.

Yahnise started throwing it back like a wild horse. "That's right baby! Fuck this pussy as if you never fucked me before! OHHHHH SHIT! I'M ABOUT TO CUMMMMMM! DON'T STOP BABY!" she said as she came again all over EJ's dick.

EJ couldn't hold it any longer so he bust right in Yahnise's pussy. "Oh shit baby! I love you so much," he said laying there with her in his arms.

Outside the door, Sonja was on the floor with her legs wide open and her boy shorts were laying on the floor next to her. She was fingering herself until she heard EJ bust and then she came at the same time. After she came, she took her fingers out of her pussy and put them in her mouth sucking the juices off, wishing it was EJ's dick. Then she jumped up and went back into her room.

* * *

At 3:00 a.m., EJ woke up thirsty. He looked over at his wife who was sleeping peacefully so he decided not to bother her. He got up with just his boxers on and went downstairs to get a soda. He had forgotten that Sonja was there.

When he got in the kitchen, Sonja was standing at the counter making a sandwich with nothing on but boy shorts and a wife beater.

"Oh shit! Excuse me. I forgot that you were here," EJ said standing there looking at her ass.

Sonja turned around and saw him standing there in only his boxers and immediately her eyes went straight to his dick. She noticed that his dick looked like it was swelling up. "I'll only be a second. I forgot to get a robe when we were out shopping earlier. I thought that you would still be knocked out after all that noise y'all were making last night," Sonja said smiling.

"My bad. I didn't know that we were that loud. I'll tone it down some. I'll be out of your way in one minute. I just came down to grab a soda," EJ said as he went to the refrigerator to grab a soda.

"I'll get it for you," Sonja said as she stepped in front of him before he could get the door open. She bent down in front of him and EJ's dick touched her ass by accident.

He jumped back and said, "Sorry, I didn't mean to do that."

She grabbed the soda and gave it to him. "Don't worry about it. Accidents happen sometimes," she said seductively.

EJ felt a surge go through his body as he looked at her camel toe through the boy shorts. When he looked down, he saw his dick at attention.

Sonja looked down and saw it also. "Damn, you better go tame that thing before it bust out of those boxers," she said laughing.

EJ covered himself up and turned to walk away when he felt Sonja grab him and turn him around. She looked at him and he looked at her. Without saying a word, Sonja scooped down on her knees, pulled his dick out, and put it in her mouth.

She started sucking his dick as if it was a lollipop. EJ grabbed her head and started fucking her mouth. He felt himself about to cum and tried to pull out, but Sonja kept his dick inside her mouth. He bust all in her mouth and she swallowed every drop.

Without saying a word, Sonja stood up, kissed him on the cheek, and went back to her room. EJ stood there trying to figure out how he had just got head from a girl that wouldn't even look in his direction back in high school. A lot of thoughts went through his mind, but the most important one was, he hoped his wife never found out.

He picked his soda up and went back upstairs. As he passed Sonja's room, he glanced in there and saw her finger fucking herself and she just stared at him the whole time. EJ stood in the doorway and watched for a couple of minutes until he saw her body shaking. He knew she had just had an orgasm. She smiled at him as he closed the door and went to his room. EJ climbed back into bed with Yahnise, put his arms around her, and went to sleep thinking about the temptation that lay in the other room.

CHAPTER 10

Making a Statement

EJ was sitting in the limo with Pedro at the West Inn parking lot in Delaware. He needed to re-up on his dope. "I'm hearing nothing but great things about this Numbers. Everyone is talking about it," Pedro said smiling at EJ.

"Hey man, what can I say... When you have the best connect in the world in your corner, you are bound to do nothing but big things," EJ said relaxing on the soft leather seats.

Pedro looked at him and shook his head. "You're being too modest, my friend. At the end of the day, I give the same product to people all over the U.S. There is something I want to talk to you about. My people have informed me that someone has been trying to purchase large quantities of heroin in the Philadelphia area. I'm a businessman, so I really hate losing money. I respect your business and you as a man with integrity, so with that being said, how would you feel about that?" Pedro said sipping his drink.

EJ was trying to study his face for any type of signs of dishonesty, but he couldn't find any. Either he was being sincere, or he was a very good liar. "Who is this person that you speak of?" EJ asked breaking the silence.

"His name is Edward Young, but you know him as Ed. From what I understand, he was your best friend the first time I started dealing with you. He came home recently and he has been out in the streets acting a fool. He will draw oo much heat on everyone so if you say yes, I will deal, but if the answer is no," Pedro said not finishing the statement.

EJ thought about it for a minute and then without hesitation he said, "Fuck him! Let him do something else!"

"That was the answer I was hoping for. Now let's get down to business. I see that you want to up your order to ten now," Pedro said.

"Yes and whatever extra you want to give me will be good also," EJ said with a smile.

"How does ten and ten sound?" Pedro asked.

"That's beautiful," EJ answered thinking about all the money he would be making now.

"Are you ready now?" Pedro asked.

"Yes I am! I have $400,000.00 in two suitcases right in the trunk of my car. Plus I have $200,000.00 in another suitcase from the last consignment, which brings the total to $600,000.00. So as you can see, I don't play with people's money," EJ said seriously.

"Well did you bring your two drivers with you?" Pedro asked.

"Yes, they are waiting for me over at the WaWa in New Castle. I didn't want them coming anywhere near this place," EJ said.

"You are a very good business associate. I really respect you a lot, and that's hard to say about people these days. Two of my guys will follow you back to New Castle in the stash cars. The third one will pull up a couple of minutes later to pick the other two up. These are your cars now, so when you come, leave them at the WaWa. My guys will then retrieve them, load them, and put them right back in the same spot. You can come straight here with the money. Here are your cars now," Pedro said looking at the two Cadillac SRZ's pull up.

"Damn! You are giving me two brand new Cadi's?" EJ asked in shock.

"Like I said before, you are a good businessman and this is my gift to you," Pedro said shaking his hand.

EJ got out the limo and watched the men grab the three suitcases out of his trunk. Then he got in his car and pulled off to go back to the WaWa to pick his boys up.

EJ has to take Chris and Loud Pack with him because ever since they had found Tuck and his girl with their brains splattered all over their car, he had lost a driver.

He didn't want to take anybody else because he didn't trust anyone else like that yet. Truth be told, EJ was glad that Tuck was dead. He was a liability to the crew.

They all had his back and were down for whatever. After EJ grabbed his crew they all headed back to Philly, three cars deeper, and twenty keys richer of pure uncut heroin.

* * *

They were all at the crib on Millick Street in the basement going over the next distribution for the product. The girls were upstairs in their thongs with a facemask and gloves on, cutting the product with the Bonita and Quad Nine.

"I just got off the phone with Trillz and he said he could do fifteen this time," Loud Pack said.

"That's great shit right there. I also have a new buyer out in D.C. His name is Bo and he wants to grab five to start off with. After he gets a chance to see what I do, he will cop more, little by little until he has the whole D.C. area on smash.

I purchased you two tickets to the Washington Wizards and Miami Heat game tomorrow night. That will give you enough time to step in B-More, and then head out to D.C. You will be sitting in the same row as the buyers. They know that you will be wearing a Philadelphia 76er's hat. After the game is over, y'all will do business. They have the money for you so that shouldn't be a problem. I want you to take Nice with you for this one. If anything goes wrong, there is enough artillery in the car to take on a mini army. You already know the codes to the stash boxes. Remember, beeping the horn will activate the stash box with the guns and the radio is for the one with the product. You still have to use all the other sequences to activate it. Any questions?" EJ asked Loud Pack.

He shook his head no, as he grabbed the two tickets from EJ. "Are we leaving tonight or tomorrow?" he asked.

"Leave tomorrow morning. That way you can splurge a little down there. I want y'all to enjoy yourselves even if you are down there on business. That way, no one will get suspicious of you," EJ said to Loud Pack and Nice.

"Now we will be giving our buildings extra work also. Instead of giving them fifty, let's give them seventy logs. Tell them to keep one hundred fifty bundles and they will owe me $11,000.00 off of the rest. That goes for all of the spots. We're eating now, but it's time to really get at it. Everybody will be rich by the summer. If my squad don't eat, neither do I," EJ said to everybody.

"So how do you want us to get everybody their shit? It only leaves me, Mel, and Sheed, with Loud Pack and Nice going out of town," Chris said knowing they had a lot of ground to cover.

"Well, I'm sending Jonay with you; Sheed and Mel can go together. Jonay earned her promotion so she's on the team now and she will ride till her death. I have Shannon and Tiff coming through also. They will hit the Delaware spots and y'all can handle out Philly and Jersey spots. Remember to be on point because Ed is out there trying to steal my shit! We already upgraded security at all the spots, but I don't trust him at all. I know what he is capable of doing," EJ said seriously to Chris.

When they were done talking, they all left for the night while Chris and the girls stayed to finish cutting the work. They turned one key into five for the D.C. buyer and they turned the rest to seven off of each one. By the time they finished that night, they had one hundred thirty eight keys.

As EJ drove home, he was really looking at how his life had changed from high school until now. He went from making $300.00 every two weeks, to becoming a millionaire from computer fraud. Now he is a multi-millionaire in the dope game. He has a beautiful wife and a handsome son. *"Damn, life is good!"* he said to himself as he jumped on the expressway heading home.

His phone started to ring bringing him back to the present. The caller ID said private, but he still answered the call anyway. "Hello," he said into the receiver.

"You have a pre-paid call from "Scrap," an inmate at a correctional facility. To accept this call, press one and wait to be connected. Thank you."

"Yo, what's up with you nigga?" EJ said excited to hear from his old celi.

"What's up playboy? I get out tomorrow and I wanted to know will you be here?" Scrap said.

"I thought you had to go back to Delaware?" EJ questioned.

"Naw, fuck them out there. I'll see them when I see them," he said as he thought about how they started shitting on him as soon as he got booked. If it weren't for EJ sending him $500.00 a week, he would be broke.

"Well, I will be up there early to get you, nigga, and we'll talk on the way home. I don't want to say too much, but you already know what time it is," EJ said.

"Okay, I'll see you in the morning," Scrap said before hanging up.

EJ knew he had a real killer coming home tomorrow. Shit was about to get turned up now and he couldn't wait either.

* * *

The next day as promised, EJ was up at CFCF on State Road waiting for Scrap to come out. Around an hour after he got there, he saw Scrap walking down the path towards him.

"Damn! They finally let your ass go," EJ said as the two shook hands and gave each other a half hug.

"Yeah and it feels good too, nigga. I thought they were going to send me upstate for that shit. I was glad that the victim said it was an accident and wouldn't testify against me. Then on top of it, they still made me sit on some other bullshit charge. Well, that's all behind me now, so what do you have planned for me?" Scrap said as they were about to hit the highway.

"You already know what's up. We about to get this money. You are on the team now. I have three shooters, but now with you, I know that shit will get done more efficiently. Look in the glove compartment. I have a gift for you in there," EJ said to Scrap.

Scrap opened the glove compartment and was greeted by a chrome Desert Eagle. "Now this is what I'm talking about," he said as he cocked it, putting one in the chamber.

"I'm glad you like it. There are two fully loaded clips in there also," EJ said.

For the rest of the ride, they listened to Rick Ross and Meek Millz. It was early so EJ decided to stop and get them something to eat at Let's Grub down the bottom (West Philly).

As they pulled up in front of the restaurant, EJ noticed one of Ed's boys conducting some business with some other man. "That's Twan right there. He works at one of Ed's spots out in North Philly. What the fuck is he doing down here?" EJ said to Scrap.

"Well, I say we find out. It's time to let these niggas know that we are for real," Scrap said with a deadly stare in his eyes.

They waited for Twan to finish talking to the dude and then they discretely followed him around the corner to the parking lot in the back of the stores. As soon as he was about to get into his car, he was greeted with two guns in his face.

"Don't fucking move, you piece of shit! What the fuck are you doing down here?" EJ asked as he snatched the bag from Twan that he was carrying. EJ noticed that it was the same kind of book bag that he gave to all of his houses.

When he opened it up, he saw money and dope. What caught his attention was the red bags with the label, "Blood Game" on it. He knew what it was now. "So you steal my shit, change the name, and then try to sell it in my territory?" EJ asked Twan.

He didn't know what to say. "Take it, man. I didn't know it was yours," was all he could get out before Scrap smacked him with his gun. He fell to the ground holding his face. "Please," Twan cried. "Please don't kill me."

"Let's go," EJ said to Scrap as he started to walk away.

Scrap kicked Twan in is face before putting a bullet in his skull.

BOOM!

The sound of the cannon was loud. Scrap reached over and hit him two more times.

BOOM!

BOOM!

All the shots were headshots, stopping his breathing immediately. Scrap and EJ ran back to the car and took off before anyone even saw them.

* * *

They were in the stash house talking about what had transpired earlier. EJ knew now that his man Scrap was about that work. He wasn't even going to kill Twan. He wanted to send a message to Ed. "Now I guess the message was loud and clear," EJ said.

"Yeah, I think you're right. Now let's see what the nigga wants to do. He tried to change the bag and name like you wouldn't find out. Now your product is out there under some "Blood Game" brand. How many spots did he hit?" Scrap asked.

"As of right now, it has only been three, but there's no telling how many more he will try to hit. That's why I added shooters on the roofs of all the houses across the street to watch everything," EJ said.

EJ went into the kitchen to make sure his new girl was doing all right. He had hired some girl by the name of Samira to replace Jonay in the lab. Felecia was jealous that she wasn't picked to do drops, but EJ knew she wasn't ready for that type of work yet.

After he checked on the girls, he went back in the room with Scrap. "So what are you doing today?" he asked him.

"I need some wheels so I can go see some people. After that, I want to go get my dick wet. It's been a minute, ya feel me," he said smiling.

"Well, just take my car," EJ said throwing him the keys. "That's your shit now. I'm going to have my wife pick me up when I'm ready to go. I'll stick around here and count the work and money with the girls."

"You don't need any help? I can stay for a while if you want," Scrap said.

"Nawwww; go ahead and take the rest of the day to catch up. Just make sure you come to the club tonight so we can party," EJ said giving him a pound. "You straight? Do you need any money?" EJ asked Scrap.

"You gave me all that money when I was booked like I could spend all that. I'm good, nigga! Thanks for the whip and I'll see you tonight," Scrap said heading for the door. He was about to go wreck some havoc on Delaware for the mutha-fuckas that were counting him out as if he wasn't going to ever come home.

* * *

When Scrap went to Delaware, the first place he stopped was on Maddison Street to see an old friend. When he turned on the block, everybody was looking at the Bentley as if it was the president. The girls that were standing out there talking to the dealers were trying to see who was in the car.

Scrap stopped right in front of the group and rolled down his window. "Yo, Dee let me holla at you real quick," he said.

The nigga Dee was surprised to see Scrap, and he looked like he wanted to shit on himself. He walked over to the car. "What's up, man? When you get out?" Dee asked nervously.

"Fuck all the small talk. Where the fuck is the money that you owe me? I bet you thought I wasn't coming home for a while, didn't you?" Scrap asked him.

"I don't have it, man. I've been out here all day long trying to make a couple of dollars. Ever since that dope hit the streets, that's all that's popping right now," Dee said.

"Well, since you don't have my money, then something has to give," Scrap said pulling out his Desert Eagle.

As soon as Dee saw the gun, he tried to run. Scrap opened the door and fired at Dee.

BOOM!

He hit Dee right in the ass. Then he jumped out the car and walked up to him aiming the gun at his head. "Get my money by next week or the next shot will be a deadly one," he said getting back in the car and pulling off while everyone else stood there with shocked looks on their faces.

Scrap's next stop was on Van Buren Street. When he got to the block, he parked on the corner. He got out and walked down the block where four dudes were playing dice. As soon as he was close enough, he pulled out his gun. "Everybody give that shit up!"

They all froze at the sight of the cannon being pointed at them. "What's this all about?" one of the dudes asked.

"Ya man right here having all of this mouth when I was down cause he thought I wasn't coming home. What? My bitch ass baby mother didn't tell you that I beat the charges?" Scrap said with venom in his voice.

When Scrap would call his daughter's mom, trying to speak to his daughter, her new nigga would always answer the phone talking shit. Now that he was home, he didn't have shit to say.

They all emptied their pockets and gave their money to Scrap. "Turn around and get on your knees," Scrap said to the four dudes. As soon as they were on their knees, Scrap hit them all in the head sending brain matter all over the place.

BOOM!

BOOM!

BOOM!

BOOM!

He knew from the sight of all of the blood, all of them would be having closed casket funerals.

Scrap ran back down the block, hopped back in the Bentley, and headed back to Philly. *"I just made a big statement to these niggas out here,"* he said to himself as he jumped on the highway.

CHAPTER 11

Robbery Gone Wrong

Gene and Ed were sitting inside of a stolen Chevy Lumina watching two of Ed's men carry two book bags into a house on Huntington Street. They had been watching the house for a couple of days now, and they wanted everything that was in there. Ed knew that it was money and drugs in those bags because this block was doing mad numbers since EJ's crew had taken over with the Heroin. Ed wanted to reclaim his block and he was going to use EJ's product to do it.

Two more of Ed's crew pulled up in another stolen car and got out. Ed and Gene cocked their guns and jumped out also. "You ready to get this money?" Ed asked as they all nodded their heads yes.

As soon as the door opened again, Ed and his crew ran up in the house and began shooting everything in sight.

POP!

POP!

POP!

POP!

BOC!

BOC!

BOC!

Ed and Gene hit the two niggas while they were trying to run. They both fell on the ground and one of Ed's goons ran over to them and put a bullet in both of their heads.

POP!

POP!

They grabbed the bags and headed out the door. When Ed looked up the block, he noticed a car had blocked off the exit. When he looked down the other end, he saw the same thing. Out of nowhere, he saw like four dudes with assault weapons headed in their direction.

"It's a setup!" Ed yelled as he took cover and started busting his gun.

POP!

POP!

POP!

POP!

Gunfire was all that could be heard for a few blocks. All hell had broken loose.

BLOCA!

BLOCA!

BLOCA!

BOC!

BOC!

BOC!

Windows and cars were being torn apart as the gunmen exchanged gunfire with each other.

Ed and his crew were pinned behind two cars that were being riddled with bullets.

They knew that they were out gunned, but they were not going out like bitches. Ed aimed his gun while lying under a car and kept firing. He hit one of the gunmen in his leg, dropping him on impact. Gene then sprung from his spot hitting another one in the head with two accurate shots.

BOC!
BOC!

As the other two were getting closer, two of Ed's men jumped up and started firing only to be shredded apart by a barrage of bullets, killing them before they even hit the ground. It was now two against two, but they had assault guns while Ed and Gene only had automatics.

Police sirens could be heard getting closer from a distance. The two gunmen retreated trying to get away before the cops came. Ed and Gene didn't have a get-away car because the two cars that they had come in were now destroyed.

As the sirens got closer, Ed saw a white van bust through the barricade that the shooters had put up. The van came to a screeching halt and a female dressed in all black jumped out of the passenger side with an AR-15 in her hand. "Let's get the fuck out of here," she yelled to Ed.

Ed and Gene ran and jumped in the van as two cops came up the block. Without even thinking twice, the female let the AR-15 rang out.

TAT!
TAT!
TAT!
TAT!
TAT!
TAT!

The police cars came to a sudden stop as the bullets hit their targets, killing the two cops in the first car while blocking the other car from getting pass. The female jumped in the van as it took off and rammed the other car that was blocking the street off.

They drove a few blocks before jumping out of the van and into a parked Jeep. The driver of the van put a rag in the gas door and lit it. Then he jumped in the Jeep and took off, as the van exploded leaving no evidence behind.

* * *

"Fuck! Fuck! Fuck! What the hell happened out there?" Ed said steaming mad that once again EJ had gotten the drop on him.

"Those niggas was ready for us. That's what the fuck happened. If it wasn't for you two, we would be dead or in jail with multiple bodies right now," Gene said looking at the male and female as they drove over the Walt Whitman Bridge heading for Jersey.

"You are one bad bitch! I sure am glad that you are on our team," Ed said to the chick as she looked out the window with her shades and hoody on.

"At least we got what we came for, but it came at a price," Gene said holding the two book bags, thinking about the two men that they had lost.

* * *

After the chick and dude dropped Ed and Gene off, they headed back to Philly before anyone missed them.

Ed and Gene went into the house to count what they had. As they walked in, Tamara was sitting on the couch watching TV in a lace panty and bra set. "Cover the fuck up! We have company," Ed said heading to the kitchen.

Tamara pulled her robe over her body as they walked pass her. Gene was staring at her the whole time. He couldn't believe Ed had turned a hoe into a housewife.

"Okay, let's count this shit up. You count the work and I'll count the money. Make sure you switch the bags to ours also," Ed said sitting at the table.

"I got you nigga. This shit that happened tonight can never happen again. Next time we go in with a whole team. That way we watch the outside, as well as the inside," Gene said.

"Yeah, you right about that. I have really underestimated this nigga. I think it's time to put Plan B into motion," Ed said counting the stacks of money.

"Are you sure you're ready to take that step? Once you cross that line, there's no turning back," Gene said.

"What other choice do I have? This nigga is starting to be a thorn in my side. I'll give it a little while longer just to see where this goes, but if he kills another member of this team, then I won't have a choice," Ed said.

"Well, being in this game, niggas are going to die. We can't live forever," Gene said as he was rewrapping the work with the Blood Game stickers.

Ed's phone rang and he answered it. He was in a deep conversation with somebody. After he hung up the phone, he got up and put his jacket on. "I'll be back in ten minutes. I have to make a quick run. When you are done, take that and put it on our new blocks. I should be back by then, but who knows," Ed said heading for the door.

"Do you want me to come with you?" Gene asked.

"Naw, I'm good. It won't take that long," Ed said and left.

* * *

Five minutes later, Ed pulled up to the Shell gas station on Highland Street. He got out of his car and got in the car with Detective Harris.

"Do you realize what the fuck you're doing? You are starting a fucking war in these streets, and body after fucking body is being found because you want to get revenge," Detective Harris said.

"It's your fucking job to lean it up. What do you think I'm paying you for?" Ed said getting mad.

"Speaking of paying, where the fuck is my money? I haven't received one payment from your ass. Don't play this fucking game with me, because you will fucking lose," he said to Ed.

In one quick motion, Ed had his gun in the detective's face. "Who are you talking to like that?" Ed asked.

"Listen man, I'm just saying that I need my money. I have shit to do just like you," Detective Harris said with his hands in the air.

"I'll have your money sent to you in the mail tomorrow. Just look outside in your mailbox when you get off," Ed said sliding out of the car and leaving.

Detective Harris knew he was becoming a problem. It's as if he made a deal with the devil. He had to figure out a way to get out of this deal. One thing he did know was, if that money were not there tomorrow, somebody would have to go.

* * *

The next day the money was in his mailbox as planned. Detective Harris still wanted to do something about Ed's wild ways. He really couldn't do too much because he had something on him. He knew that Detective Harris had committed murder for money. With that dark secret lingering in the air, he decided to get both Ed and EJ to kill each other. He just had to figure out how he would do it.

CHAPTER 12

First but Not Last

It was 3:00 a.m. when EJ made it home from checking on his other spots. When he received the call saying a couple of his men had been killed in a robbery, he headed straight to Philly. He was getting tired of Ed now, and it was time for him to send his people out. That's exactly what he was going to do at the meeting tomorrow.

EJ went upstairs to check on his family. First, he went into his son's room and he was sleeping peacefully. Next, he went to see what Yahnise was doing. He walked passed Sonja's door and it was closed. When he went into his room, his wife was sleeping so he headed back downstairs.

After making himself a sandwich, he went into the living room, sat on the couch, and started to watch TV. Even though he was tired, he still couldn't go straight to bed without watching the news. He turned the TV on and the first thing he saw was a reporter talking about the high percentage of people overdosing off of this new drug called Numbers.

"Damn! I have to cut that shit some more," EJ said to himself.

He listened a little longer and then he started channel surfing. When he got to Cinemax, House Party was on so he starting watching that. He leaned back on the couch and dosed off.

"Wake up and go to bed," Sonja said waking EJ up.

He looked up at Sonja wearing a robe and slippers. "Oh shit! I didn't even know that I had fallen asleep. What are you doing up and what time is it?" EJ said.

"Its 4:05 and I was going to make me a sandwich, but beings though you didn't touch yours, I'll just take this one," she said as she took a bite of his sandwich and sat down next to him.

EJ had been keeping his distance since that night in the kitchen. He didn't want to get caught doing anything crazy, especially while his wife was in the house.

"Oh shit, you are down here watching G-string Diva's. I'm telling Yahnise," Sonja said playing with him.

"Ha, ha, ha. For your info, I was watching House Party until I fell asleep. This shit do be jumping though. Look at their bodies," EJ said as they watched the show.

"Shit, me and my girl would put their bodies to shame, and she had a baby," Sonja said standing up imitating the girl on the TV.

EJ laughed at her and pulled her down on the couch. "Sit your butt down. You are crazy," he said noticing that her robe had come open. She was completely naked underneath it.

"See something you like? If you do, then come get it," she said as she put one leg up on the couch exposing her neatly trimmed pussy. "Ever since that night that I saw you and Yahnise making love, I have wanted to see how your dick felt inside of me. I swear I won't say anything. It will be our little secret."

EJ was shocked that she had seen them fucking. "I don't know about that. We went too far the last time," he said still watching her as she stuck her finger in her pussy and then put it in EJ's mouth.

"Taste this and tell me that you don't want it," she said as she pulled her finger in and out of his mouth. His tongue licked all of her juices off of her finger.

Then she started unbuckling his belt. She pulled his dick out, bent down, and took him in her mouth.

After a couple of minutes, EJ pushed her head off of him, stood up, and fixed his clothes. "I can't do this. My wife and your friend is right upstairs sleep," he said feeling guilty.

Sonja got up and grabbed his hand. "Follow me," she said as they headed towards the basement. EJ reluctantly let her led him down the stairs. When they got down in the basement, she pushed EJ into one of the walls and pulled his pants down. This time he didn't stop her. He closed his eyes and enjoyed the feeling.

After a couple of minutes of sucking his dick, Sonja needed to feel him inside of her. "EJ, I want you to fuck me real good, right now," she said as she got up and let her robe fall to the ground exposing her damn near perfect body.

EJ couldn't deny how beautiful her body was. He walked over, took two pillows off of the couch, and placed them on the floor. Sonja walked over and helped him take off the rest of his clothes. She couldn't believe how ripped his body was.

EJ gently pushed her down on the pillows and pinned one of her legs down while putting her other leg on his shoulder as he went deep inside of her.

"Ohhhh shit! Mmmmmmmm! Give it to me, Daddy!" Sonja said out loud, as she grabbed his ass and made him pump faster.

She kept making loud noises, so EJ kept stopping telling her to be quiet. He even started kissing her to keep her from screaming. He knew she couldn't take too much dick, but he kept drilling her on purpose. He was trying to knock her back out. Sonja's pussy was so tight that he had to open her legs up real wide for his dick to penetrate her slippery walls.

Her pussy was so good, that he came inside of her and kept pumping trying to get another one off before they stopped.

"Oh God!" she hollered as he started moving in circular motions.

Then he lifted her up with ease, while still inside of her and sat on the couch letting her ride him. It seemed as if his dick was in her stomach the way she was screaming.

EJ knew he couldn't keep going too much longer or they would get caught.

She slowly started rocking back and forth, as she came for the second time all over his dick. It was running down her inner thighs, all over his balls.

EJ felt his nut building up again so he stood up and bent her over the couch and started punishing her from the back.

"Yessss E! Oh my fucking God! You are killing me!" she gasped.

As soon as EJ was about to bust, he pulled out and put it all over her ass. So much cum came out this time that he could have filled up a cup. "Damn girl, if I wasn't married, I would have to wife you," EJ said laughing.

"Shut up and go wash up before you get in bed with Yahnise. If she smells you right now, she will kill you," Sonja said as she put her robe back on.

"For real though, we cannot do this again. I don't want to lose my wife like that. If she catches us, it will be a wrap," EJ said while washing up over at the sink in the basement.

"I don't know if I will be able to find someone who can fuck me like you just did, but I will try," she said as she kissed him on the lips and grabbed his dick feeling it getting hard again. "Let me leave you alone," she said smiling and then she left.

While Sonja walked upstairs to her room, she thought to herself, *"Nigga, I know you came in me the first time. I better not be pregnant or I will be breaking up a happy home."*

* * *

The next morning, EJ left our early so he could meet up with his team. It was time to start hitting Ed's houses as he had done his. He didn't want anybody to think that they could do what they wanted with no repercussions. It was time to pay the piper.

When he pulled up to the crib on Millick Street, he noticed that even Shannon and Tiff's cars were already out there. He walked in the door and everybody had on all black army fatigues. They had on bulletproof vest and each one had an AK-47 or an AR-15. From the looks on their faces, he could tell that they all knew it was time to kill.

"Now that we are all here, I would like to start off by saying that each and every last one of y'all now have over $50,000.00 in your account. When you get the time, check it out. That doesn't go for you two, Shannon and Tiff. You both know what's up with y'alls. This is how we are going to do this. Ed has a spot on Diamond Street, Kensington, and Toresdale, and one on 22nd and Mckean. So we are going to hit all of them at the same time. Kill every fucking body in there. I don't want anybody walking up out of there alive," EJ said with authority.

"So what are the teams on this?" Tiff asked as she fixed her hoody.

"How many young boys do we have ready to roll out?" EJ asked looking at Chris who had picked them out.

"We have thirty goons all outside ready to roll out. I have six in three different vans and four in three different cars. So it will be one van and one car at each spot," Chris said.

"Okay, so Shannon you will drive a van. Tiff and Scrap, y'all will drive one of the other vans. Nice and Mel will lead the crew to Diamond Street. Sheed and Loud Pack, y'all hit the crib out in Kensington, and me and Chris will hit McKean Street.

I'm hoping that Ed is in one of these muth-fuckas, cause I'm tired of his ass," EJ said hitting his fist together.

"Okay, let's handle our business," EJ said as they all loaded up in the vans and cars and headed for their respective destinations.

* * *

When EJ and his goons pulled up on 22nd and McKean, they all threw their hoodies on and jumped out of the van and car. "Hit everything," EJ said as they went through the block shooting.

BLAKA!

BLAKA!

BLAKA!

TAT!

TAT!

TAT!

POP!

POP!

POP!

All that could be seen was random people dropping like flies. They were hitting everyone, even the kids. It was total devastation on the block. Even though EJ felt bad about the kids that had fell victim to this madness, he felt as though he was making a statement that said everybody could get it.

"Let's get the fuck out of here!" Chris yelled as everybody started running back to the van and car.

At that moment, a car came speeding down the block. It stopped and Ed jumped out busting his Riot Pump.

BOOM!

BOOM!

BOOM!

EJ was the last one to the van when he caught two bullets to his chest. He fell before he could get in the van.

"EJ!" Chris yelled as he jumped out letting off.

BLOCA!

BLOCA!

BLOCA!

At that time, the four goons jumped out and started shooting at Ed and the driver.

Ed ducked behind a car and kept firing until his shells ran out. When they ran out, he pulled out his 40 caliber and started letting off.

BOC!

BOC!

BOC!

Christ had got EJ in the van, and they pulled off getting the fuck out of there. EJ's goons were holding Ed off until they got around the corner.

The four goons then jumped in the car and pulled off. Ed ran out and started busting his gun at the car.

The car's windows shattered and then swerved and hit another car. Ed kept firing aiming for the gas tank.

BOC!

BOC!

BOC!

CLICK! CLICK!

The car burst into flames exploding killing all four people inside just as he ran out of bullets.

Ed jumped back in the car as the driver took off. They made it around the corner before the whole first district came around the corner.

That carnage left eighteen bodies dead in the street. Out of the eighteen, two of them were little kids that were no older than ten. All of Ed's workers were dead and four of EJ's workers were causalities of war also. Three of the other bodies were people who were just outside walking in the wrong area at the wrong time. This war was really getting serious between the two men. It was survival of the fittest. Who was going to come out on top?

* * *

EJ was laying in the van in a lot of pain. He had taken two pump shots to the vest that he was wearing. A couple of pellets caught him in his left arm. The impact of the blast is what knocked him off his feet. There was so much blood coming from his arm that it looked like he was hit in several spots.

"Hang in there, EJ. We'll get you taken care of in a few minutes," Chris said as he placed a shirt over the wound and kept pressure on it.

"I'm calling Tasha now to let her know that we are on our way there," Shannon said as she headed to Southwest.

Tasha was a nurse at the University Hospital. She also did side jobs for people who couldn't go into the emergency room. She and EJ were cousins so she was always on call whenever he needed her. It didn't matter what time of day or night it was, she was only a phone call away. He paid her real good, so there was never a problem when he needed her.

When they pulled up to Tasha's crib, she was already waiting on them. "Take him straight to the basement," she said to Shannon and Chris.

They helped EJ downstairs and put him on the operating table. Tasha quickly took his vest and shirt off so that she could try to stop the bleeding. She gave him an anesthetic for the pain. After cleaning the wound, she stitched him up and wrapped a bandage around it

"There you go, crybaby. Take some Motrin if the pain comes back. Other than that, you should heal and be back to your old self in a week or two," Tasha said cleaning the mess up.

"Cuz, that's why you are my favorite," EJ said while she helped him put on a clean shirt that she had got from her boyfriend.

After paying her, they left so that they could make sure the rest of the team had made it back okay. Chris had called Jonay and told her to come pick them up. The goons had left them there so they could get rid of the van.

EJ was pissed that Ed had tried to kill him. Even though he knew they were at war, a small part of him wanted to believe that Ed would come around.

"I guess this nigga really wants me dead," EJ said to himself.

CHAPTER 13

Vacation

A month went by from when EJ and Ed had their shootout. Ed had taken off to Miami until the heat died down some. He figured by the time he came back, everything would be back to normal and he could execute the next part of his plan.

Ed wasn't worried about his blocks making money. The only thing that was on his mind was making EJ's life a living hell. Deep down inside, Ed was jealous of EJ. He came home and truly blew up in the drug game. EJ never knew how to sell a five-dollar cap, and now he was selling weight of dope all over their city and other cities too. Plus, he has the baddest girl in Philly as his wife and a son with her.

All of those things and the fact that he killed Ed's mom, was enough to drive a person like Ed to the point of no return.

Ed and Tamara were at the Marriott Hotel on Ocean Drive. They were on the beach enjoying the sun. Ed had brought Gene along because he didn't want anything to happen to him while they were gone. Gene was flirting with these two white girls who were laying on towels trying to get a tan.

"Look at that nigga playing Mack Daddy with the snow bunnies," Ed said as he rubbed baby oil on Tamara's back and butt.

"I know the only macking you better be doing is with me," Tamara said sucking her teeth.

Ed squeezed her ass. "You know it's me and you against the world, Ma. Now turn over so I can put some oil on your stomach," he said.

Tamara turned over and sat up so she could take a sip of her drink. "Are we still going to hit the club scene tonight? They have this reggae band playing at the club in our hotel and I want to go," she said puckering up her lips.

"Yes, we are still going to the club. Besides, I have to meet one of the people that's going to supply me with Perks and Mollies," Ed said.

They sat out enjoying the ocean breeze and sand for about two hours before they headed back to their hotel room to get ready for the club scene. Ed and Tamara's room was right next to Gene's room so if anything popped off, they would be close to each other. Ed had a swipe card to both rooms because Gene kept the guns in the room with him. They were going to go over to the club at nine, so they had a few hours to rest up. As soon as they laid down, both Ed and Tamara drifted off to sleep in each other's arms.

***

They arrived at the club after nine and it was jammed packed. The reggae band had everyone on the floor dancing. Ed, Tamara, and Gene made their way over to the VIP section. Even though Ed came to enjoy himself, he still had business to handle.

The waitress came over and gave them their drinks. Gene pulled out a hundred bill for the waitress and stuck it down in her bra. That was just her tip. "Maybe we can get together later," he told her. She just smiled and walked away. Gene was already high from all of the loud he had puffed before they came to the club. Now he was drinking and trying to hit on every female with a skirt.

Ed laughed as he watched his boy have a good time. Out here, they didn't have a care in the world. There was no killing or worrying about this or that. They could put up their feet and just have fun. Ed still stayed on point just in case though. Wherever you went, you still had haters.

Just a little after eleven, the man Ed was waiting for sent the waitress over to inform him that he was ready to see him. "I'll be back in a few minutes baby. Enjoy yourself and only get one more drink," Ed said as he followed the lady to an office in the back.

Tamara waited for Ed to leave before she reached in her purse and took out two Mollies that she had purchased from the waitress earlier. She wanted to spice their sexual appetite up for the night. She knew that the pills would kick her into overdrive and she would want to fuck all night long. She took the pills and popped them in her mouth. Then she finished off her drink before ordering two more.

***

Ed walked into the office and was greeted by an older white man. With all of his grey hair, Ed assumed the older man was in his sixties. "How are you? Have a seat," the man said standing to shake Ed's hand. After he shook his hand, he motioned for Ed to have a seat.

"My name is Tony. I'm the one that spoke to you briefly on the phone. My associate has informed me that you are interested in purchasing Mollies and Perks. How much do you want to order?" Tony said getting straight to business.

Ed thought about it for a minute, trying to figure out a good number. When he couldn't come up with anything, he said," Make me an offer that I can't refuse."

Tony smiled at his answer. "Smart man. I will give you ten thousand Perks for sixty thousand dollars and I'll even throw in one thousand Molly pills for an additional five grand. Does that sound like something you want to hear?" he said.

"I'll take that deal, but I'll give you an extra ten grand for two thousand Mollies. I came too far not to take back as much as I can," Ed said.

"We have a deal, my friend. I will phone the supplier and have him deliver it here. I want you to stay put and wait for me so that we can talk arrangements," Tony said.

"No problem. Just have one of your waitresses tell my wife that I'll meet her back at the hotel room," Ed said, as he got comfortable in his seat.

***

After Tamara finished getting her drink on, she decided that it was time to get her freak on with her husband. She was feeling really horny and her pussy was tingling in anticipation of what was to come when she got upstairs. The waitress had sent her the swipe cards from Ed so she could get in. She stumbled to the elevator and got on heading to her room.

When she got to her room, she swiped the keycard and went in. She saw her man lying on the bed asleep. She wondered how in the hell did he get up here without coming to get her. Right about now, she really didn't care about anything else besides fucking her boo. Her pussy was so wet that her juices were threatening to run down her legs. On the short ride in the elevator, she had been massaging her clit under her dress. She didn't have on any panties so she was really working her clit overtime in the elevator.

It was dark in the room so Tamara decided to creep over to the bed and give Ed a surprise wake up present. She slipped out of her dress and crawled in the bed butt naked.

Tamara pulled his shorts off and grabbed his dick, putting it in her mouth. The warm sensation of Tamara's mouth caused him to wake up. He couldn't believe how good her mouth felt on his dick.

"Mmmmmm baby, damn this feels good," he said moving her head up and down on his dick.

Tamara wanted some dick now. She slowly slid up his stomach, put her pussy in line with his dick, and then slowly eased down on it. The pleasure had her in another world. She thought he wasn't all the way hard because it didn't feel the way it should, but she thought it was due to him being sleep.

She started riding the shit out of his dick. "Ummmm, yes baby!" Tamara whispered in sexual bliss as she bit her bottom lip preparing to explode.

When Tamara came all over his dick, he felt himself about to bust also. "Let me hit this pussy from the back. I always wanted to fuck you," he said flipping her over trying to hit it doggy style.

Those comments made Tamara start to think… *"I always wanted to fuck you,"* she played back over again in her head. It hit her like a ton of bricks as he entered her from behind.

Tamara quickly jumped up off the bed and ran over to the light switch. When she turned the light on, her heart almost jumped out of her chest.

Laying on the bed butt naked was Ed's friend Gene. Tamara was so horny that she didn't even notice the difference of the person she was fucking. She quickly covered herself up with one of the sheets.

"What are you doing in our room?" she asked him.

Gene looked like he wanted to laugh, but instead he said, "I came in here drunk and fell asleep. I thought you knew it was me."

"Hell no! I didn't! You need to get the fuck out of here before Ed gets back!" she yelled covering up more tightly.

Gene got up with his dick in his hand and walked towards Tamara. "Come on Ma, let's finish this. You know you was feeling good from all this dick," he said pulling the sheet from her body.

Tamara was still horny, but she couldn't do it. She moved trying to get away, but he grabbed her and pushed her on the edge of the bed. He lift her legs up in the air and entered her wet pussy again.

She tried to resist, but the Mollies had her wanting more. She started fucking him back like a wild animal.

After Gene came inside of her, she said, "Leave now before Ed comes in her and kills us both."

"Meet me at my room so we can finish this," he said putting on his shorts and shirt, and then leaving out of her room.

Tamara wanted some more dick and even though he wasn't as big as Ed, he still was effective. She picked up her phone and called Ed to ask him when he was coming up. He told her that he would be about another hour. She was mad because this was supposed to be their time together.

Tamara hung up the phone and said, "Fuck it! I'm going to get this appetite fulfilled." She grabbed her robe and headed next door to Gene's room. She thought that she could be back by the time Ed got back.

***

Ed came back to his room sooner than he thought. He and Tony had made all of the arrangements, so now it was time to celebrate with his wife. When Ed entered his room and cut on the lights, he noticed that the bed was messed up. He called out Tamara's name, but got no answer.

He decided to head next door to Gene's room to see if he had seen her. He had the swipe card so he didn't need to knock.

As soon as he walked in the door, a rush of anger hit him as he saw his wife laying on the bed while Gene was eating her pussy. They both jumped when she saw Ed.

Before either one of them could say anything, Ed pulled out his 40 caliber and lit both of them up like the Fourth of July. He was so full of rage that he didn't stop squeezing the trigger until he heard the clicking sound from the empty gun.

Tamara and Gene's lifeless bodies ended up back in the oral position with blood everywhere.

Ed quickly ran to the closet, grabbed the bag with the guns, and left the room. He went back to his room and packed up everything of his and Tamara's before quickly leaving the hotel.

He called Tony and told him that he needed to grab his shit now so that he could head back home. He told him that he had an emergency. Once they met up and did their business, Ed was on the road back to Philly.

"From now on, I only trust me! I knew I shouldn't have ever tried to turn a ho into a housewife," Ed thought as he headed down I-95. His vacation had to end early because he had just murdered his wife and right hand man. Now he had to figure out what he was going to do with all the pills he had purchased.

Ed thought about it for a few minutes while he listened to Sheek Louch and decided to sell it out of the house next door. He figured that he would be able to control the whole block and supply them with anything that they needed.

When Ed pulled up in a gas station to fill up his tank, he couldn't help but to think about the chain of events that had just taken place. He wondered how long it would be before the cops connected the murders back to him. As he moved Tamara's bag out of the way looking for his sunglasses, he noticed an envelope sticking out of her bag with doctor's letterhead on it.

Ed grabbed it and seen that it had already been opened so he took the letter out and read it. The letter said that Tamara was six weeks pregnant. Ed hit the steering wheel a few times wondering how he had just killed his unborn child and the mother to be. This was something that was going to haunt him for the rest of his life.

CHAPTER 14

Problem Solved

In North Philly, Detective Harris and EJ sat outside one of his spots talking. "I already cut our product once. If I cut it anymore, it will be garbage," Ed said sitting in the car.

"Well you need to do something because bodies after bodies are turning up on these streets because of your damn near raw dope that you are putting out. Pretty soon, you will have the Drug Enforcement Agency (DEA) trying to shut shit down. If that happens, not only will it be fucking with your money, but mines as well. I refuse to let that shit go down, so do what you need to do and do it fast," Detective Harris said.

Lately a lot of fiends had been dying because of the potency of the dope. It was all over the local news channels several of times a day. EJ knew if it made the world news, the DEA would be sure to investigate soon. His back was in a corner so he wasn't going to let that happen.

"Okay, I will tell my lab workers to cut it some more. At least I will be making more money from it," EJ said giving in to what Detective Harris had said.

"So will I still be seeing you on Friday? It will be the beginning of the month. I want to buy myself some new golf clubs," Detective Harris said smirking.

"I'll give you a call when I'm ready to meet you," EJ said getting out of the car and shutting the door.

Detective Harris rolled down the window and said, "I get off of work at five, so hit me up after that time. I will be waiting."

EJ put his middle finger up as the detective drove off down the street.

***

"I need you to cut this some more and cut the rest also," EJ said passing the girls logs that he had retrieved from a couple of spots.

"What about the new shipment that is still in the stash boxes out in the cars?" Felicia asked. She had been trying to get back in good with EJ since he had only been dealing with her on a business level. They hadn't fucked since that night at the hotel. She also noticed how Jonay and he had been closer since that night. She was actually getting jealous because Jonay was stealing all of the shine. She tried to keep her feelings under wraps for now, though.

"I want you to cut the new shipment into twelve instead of seven. We've been having some major problems even out in D.C. I'm going to take ten of that out to Williamsport tonight. I have a buyer out there ready to spend a nice grip. I will be in the other room making some calls. Let me know after you are done with that so I can get on the road," EJ said to Felicia.

"Okay, but we are running low on Quad nine. We have enough for this shipment, but we will need it for the next one," she said.

"I got you," EJ said leaving the girls to handle their business. He went into the living room and called Scrap.

"What's up E?" Scrap said on the third ring.

"I need you to take a trip with me out to Williamsport to see a crib," EJ said using codes to let him know that he needed him to go with him to make a drop.

"Where are you at? I can come meet you now," Scrap said.

"I'll be here at the spot for a while. Just come straight here and we'll go now so we can hurry and get back," EJ told him before ending the call.

Next, he made a call to Yahnise. "Hey beautiful, what are you doing?" EJ said.

"Hey yourself! I'm at the club right now finishing up some paperwork that I have accumulated over the last couple of days. Why, is everything okay?" she said in a worried tone.

"Yes, everything is fine. Can't a man call his other half without something being wrong? Don't answer that, big head. Anyway, I will be heading out of town, but I'll be back hopefully before the club closes tonight. Do you want me to pick you up from there or will you be driving yourself home?" he asked.

"Actually I will be with Sonja so I'll just meet you at home. We are going to leave early because I have to get Ziaire from my mom's house. She has another doctor's appointment tomorrow morning. Nyia and Chris will be closing for me, so just take care of your business and I'll see you when you get home," Yahnise said while typing keys on her computer.

"Okay, I'll see you later. I love you baby girl," EJ said.

"I love you too," she said before hanging up.

After hanging up, EJ went to see if the girls were ready for him. He had begun to trust them so much now that they didn't have to walk around naked anymore, even though they didn't mind.

Once they were finished with what he needed, he took it out to the Cadillac SRX and put it away in the stash box. While he was doing that, Scrap pulled up on the other side of the street.

"I'm ready whenever you are," he said giving EJ a pound.

"Okay, let's roll out now then. I will drive down, but you are driving back," EJ said as they got in the car and pulled off.

"I got that new Rick Ross and Jeezy. You have to hear this shit," Scrap said putting his gun in the stash spot before plugging his iPhone into the car stereo.

They rode listening to the new track over and over, while Scrap sat back and smoked his Loud.

***

A few hours later, they were in Williamsport. They were supposed to meet the new buyer at Brown University. After talking to him and letting him know where they were, they went straight to the college.

The purpose of this trip was to establish some clientele out here as they had everywhere else. Since the guy talked to EJ and only wanted to do business with him, he had to come himself. He brought Scrap along to make sure nothing happened.

They sat in the University parking lot for about fifteen minutes before a candy apple-red Escalade pulled up beside them. The driver and passenger got out and stood there looking at EJ and Scrap. EJ and Scrap both exited their car and walked half way to meet them.

The man they were meeting was named Sean. He was about six feet, nine inches tall, very thin, and he looked like he played basketball. That's why he went to this college, EJ thought to himself.

They all greeted each other and got down to business. "I have ten of those things for you if you can handle it. I'm going to give it to you for $60,000.00 a key. Once you cut it, you will make that back off of one-half of them. Right now you owe me six hundred thousand dollars," EJ said to the college kids.

"Trevor grab the money for them," Sean said watching his friend grab the money and bring it over. "It's all there. You can count it if you want. I will wait," he said.

Scrap went over to the Caddi to count the money. After he counted all of the money, he gave them the work. Scrap threw the money-counting machine back in the stash box.

"Why don't you fellas stick around for a while and come to our frat party? There will be plenty of girls and liquor there," Sean said being polite.

As much as they wanted to, they had to get back to the city of brotherly love. "Maybe next time. We have a lot of shit going on right now," EJ said shaking their hands.

"Suit yourselves. Just trying to be hospitable," Sean said jumping back in the Escalade along with Trevor and pulling off. They stopped and backed up rolling the windows down. "We'll be ready again next month. See you then," Sean said pulling back off.

They didn't know how close they were to getting aired out as Scrap put the Tech-9 back under his jacket while they got in their car.

As soon as they hit the turnpike, EJ received a call from Nice. "Yo, what's up?"

"I'm sorry to be disturbing you, but I'm over my shorty's crib out here in Jersey and guess who is in a car talking at the gas station?" he asked.

"Well I don't feel like playing any guessing games so give it to me straight," EJ said listening carefully.

"That no good ass Detective Harris is conversing with Ed right now. They've been here for a while. At first I didn't know who they were until Ed got out the car and gave him an envelope which looked like it was cash," Nice said.

EJ was boiling. "That no good mutha-fucka is making deals with the enemy. I should have known. Thanks man. I will see you later," EJ said.

"If you want, I'll take care of both of their grimy asses right now," Nice said cocking his gun.

"Naw, let them breath for now. Enjoy the rest of your night with your shorty," EJ said hanging up.

He looked over to his friend Scrap, "We might have a problem amongst us. Let's get back to figure this shit out," he said as Scrap cruised down the turnpike back to Philly.

CHAPTER 15

Caught In the Act

It had been a month since the murder of Ed's wife and worker. Since then, so much had changed in his life. Now he was smoking Wet, snorting Coke, and being very promiscuous with the ladies. That was his remedy for keeping Tamara off of his mind.

Every day, Ed would go out and rob people just for the hell of it. He didn't need the money because he had millions in his offshore account. He was just starting to become a loose cannon and no one wanted to deal with him. Even his Perk connect discontinued their business with him after learning why he left so fast from Miami.

Ed's sister Erica called him once a week just to check on him. She had moved to Atlanta to be with her up-and-coming rapper boyfriend. His music was blowing up the airwaves and she wanted to reap the benefits of it.

"Mmmm damn, I had fun last night," the chocolate beauty said as she got up and put her clothes on. "Call me later if you want to meet up again. I have to go to work now and I won't be off until about eight."

"Damn, can a nigga get some early morning head before you go," Ed said snorting a line of Coke off the mirror.

"Well, only five minutes," she said climbing no he bed and taking Ed's dick into her mouth.

"That's what I'm talking about," Ed said as he closed his eyes enjoying the girls head game.

***

After Ed got dressed, he headed out to check on some of his spots. His Perk 30's were doing great for him. He had the Mollies being sold at all the area college parties. He was running out of product though. It pissed him off that his connect had cut him off. There was a time when Ed thought about going out there just to murk his ass. Reality kicked in though, because if he had went out there, they would surely lock him up. His picture had been posted on the news as a "Person of Interest."

The police had looked at the surveillance tape from the hotel, and posted the video footage of Ed leaving the room on every news channel. It only made The World News once. That's how Ed saw it.

Ed pulled up in Karmen Suite Apartment's and met up with his new Lieutenant, Ty. He had met Ty about a year ago. Ty was a coldhearted killer just like Ed, so the two meshed real well together.

Ty was from North Philly, but he wanted to get away from there. He decided to move to Southwest and take over some spots for Ed.

"How's business going out here?" Ed asked the young boy.

He didn't even respond. He just sat the bag of money in Ed's lap and smiled. "Does that answer your question?" he said.

"How much is in here?" Ed asked looking inside.

"It's about forty thousand in there. I will have more by this time tomorrow. I'm going to Cheyenne College tonight and knock the rest of the pills off. Those college girls love that shit," Ty said smiling.

"Good because I'm going to try to find a new connect out here somewhere. I may not get the same prices, but at least we will have product," Ed said.

"Alright, let me get back in here with this shorty. You be safe out in these streets," Ty said giving Ed a fist bump.

Ty got out of the car and looked around before heading back in the crib. He knew that Ed had been out here on some bullshit, so he was always cautious whenever he was around. He didn't want to get caught slipping because of Ed's beef.

Ed pulled off thinking about what he was going to do for the day. When he got out of the apartment complex, he pulled over to the side of the road to snort a line of Coke and to light up some Wet. He was becoming addicted to the drugs, and now he needed something to do to release some tension. He decided to go out to look for another victim to rob.

***

"What the hell took you so long to get here? I've been calling your phone for the last hour. We have a lot of shit to cut today and I need all of my lab workers here on time," Loud Pack said to Samira as she walked in the door.

"I had to stop at the bank first. We do have a life outside of this, you know," she said with her hands on her hips.

EJ had put Loud Pack in charge of all the cutting and distribution of the work. That was all he had to do and he was eating lovely off of it.

"If you don't want to be here, then you can get the fuck out! I can find some other bitch to take your place!" Loud Pack said getting up in Samira's face as if he was ready to smack her.

Samira knew she wouldn't find another job that paid her as good as this one did. She had dropped out of high school when she was in the tenth grade. That resulted in her selling her pussy and stripping. She really didn't want to go back to that life. Samira figured that she could save up and go back to school so that she could do something real with her life. She needed this money so she swallowed her pride.

"I apologize for talking to you like that. Can I please keep my job?" she asked.

Loud Pack just looked at her for a minute and then he told her to get to work. Samira left her purse on the couch and went to help the girls.

Loud Pack was sitting on the couch watching Kevin Hart's standup comedy when he heard a phone go off. He looked around to see where it was coming from when it went off again. He moved Samira's purse and noticed that she had left it there. He picked up the phone and saw that she had a text message. He decided to be nosey and read her text message. When he saw the caller's name, he damn near jumped up off the couch. The text message said:

Hey girl, I need some more of that bomb head you got. Meet me tonight at the same place that we linked up at last night

The message was from Ed.

Loud Pack dropped the phone on the couch and pulled out his phone to call EJ. His phone kept ringing so he texted him, *"911"* and waited.

About two minutes later, Loud Pack's phone began to ring. It was EJ so he immediately answered. "You need to get to the house ASAP. One of our girls is working with the other team," he said not wanting to say too much on the phone.

"Say no more! I'll be there in thirty minutes. Keep your eyes open," EJ said before he hung up.

***

When EJ got to the house, he went straight to the room where Loud Pack was. He didn't even speak to any of the girls. "What you got for me?" he asked getting to the point.

Loud Pack showed him the text that was sent to Samira. He had forwarded it to his phone after he hung up with EJ and then deleted the forwarded message out of her phone so she wouldn't know that he had seen it.

"Do you think she has been saying anything?" EJ asked him.

"I don't know. She came here late today saying that she had stopped off at the bank, but the text message says she was with him," Loud Pack said.

"Don't say anything about this to anybody. When she leaves tonight, we are going to follow her. Hopefully she will lead us straight to this nigga," EJ said.

"I'm going to watch her and make sure she's not taking any of our product to that mutha-fucka also. That's probably how he was knowing when to hit our spots.

"I'll take the blame for that. I should have did my homework on her before I let her in this organization. This will be the last time I make that mistake," EJ vowed as they went to the basement to watch the monitors that he had installed earlier.

***

Samira had just left the stash house and was heading to meet up with Ed. She had texted him back and told him that she was on her way. She had no idea that she had company (two cars) behind her.

EJ and Loud Pack were in all black in a squatter following Samira. "You think she is going there now?" Loud Pack asked loading the AK-47.

"Yeah, I called Wan and told him to program my phone to get the same calls and text messages as she does. Look, she just told him that she's on her way," EJ said showing Loud Pack the text.

"That fucking Wan is a genius on that damn computer shit. I didn't know you stayed in touch with him," Loud Pack said remembering all the good shit EJ had told him about Wan.

"Yeah, that's still my partner. He went back to his country to be with his family. I wish he was still here though," EJ said.

Samira pulled up to a house on 63rd and Carpenter Street. It was in a secluded part of West Philly. When she got out of the car, she texted Ed to let him know that she was outside. He texted back immediately informing her that the door was already open and she walked right in closing it behind her.

"You ready?" EJ asked as he cocked that AK back and pulled his mask down over his face.

"Let's get this nigga," Loud Pack said doing the same.

They jumped out of the car and headed for the house. One of them went to the front of the house while the other one went to the back.

"Come here girl and dance for me," Ed said sitting on the couch.

Samira took off her coat and started stripping while R-Kelly played in the background. As soon as she bent down to pull her panties off; a barrage of bullets rang out.

CLAK!

CLAK!

CLAK!

CLAK!

CLAK

CLAK!

CLAK!

Gunfire was all that could be heard, as windows shattered and things started breaking.

Samira stood up and started screaming, but she was immediately silenced for life as bullets riddled her naked body to pieces.

Ed stayed low and crawled to the basement door. Once he got through the door, he ran down the stairs and went through the secret door that he had installed. It led him to the abandoned house next door. He didn't know how many people were out there. All he knew was it sounded like World War II back in there.

Once their clips were empty, they ran back to the car and jumped in. EJ sped off not even checking to see if he had hit his intended target.

"I hope we got his ass," Loud Pack said sparking up a Dutch.

Ed looked out the window of the abandoned house as the car sped down the street. He didn't know who the passenger was, but he damn sure knew who the driver was. "I'm going to get all of y'all if it's the last thing that I do!" he said as he ran back to his house to get some of his stuff and leave.

He had been staying there ever since Tamara's death. Now he had to find a new spot and he knew just who to call.

**

After EJ dropped Loud Pack off at his car, he headed home. When he walked in the door, Sonja and Yahnise were watching the news. "Hey, what are you two still doing up?" he said leaning down and giving his wife a kiss.

"We were watching the news. Looks like somebody house got caught in the middle of a war. When the cops searched the house, they found a female body shot up with over fifty bullets from a big powerful gun," Yahnise said as she moved over and let EJ sat on the couch between her and Sonja.

"Damn! That's crazy," EJ said frustrated that it was only one body found in the house instead of two.

"Are you hungry? I made some fried chicken and mac & cheese," Yahnise said as she got up to make him a plate.

"You know I am," he said smacking her on the ass.

As soon as Yahnise went into the kitchen, Sonja grabbed EJ's dick. "I'm hungry too! Are you gonna meet me in the basement tonight?" she said as she rubbed his dick until it got hard.

EJ moved her hand. "I don't know if I can do that tonight," he said moving over a little putting some distance in between the both of them.

They had been sneaking around for a while now, but EJ was tired of doing it. He didn't know how to tell her that he didn't want to do it anymore, so he had been avoiding an encounter with her for the last two weeks.

"Damn, you acting like you don't want any more of this sweet pussy. What's up with that?" she questioned.

"Like I said, I'm chilling tonight so can you just drop it?" EJ said.

"I'll be in there in a few minutes with your food baby, unless you want me to bring it up to our bedroom," Yahnise said from the kitchen.

"Yeah, bring it upstairs. I'm going to check on little man," EJ said getting up.

Sonja looked at him crazy and then said, "Well, if you want me tonight, just knock on my door and I'll be there." She stuck her hand inside of her tights and started fingering herself while looking at EJ.

EJ stared at her for about thirty seconds and then he went upstairs to check on his son. He couldn't believe that Sonja was starting to act like that. From that point on, EJ had decided to end this little affair he had going on with Sonja.

Yahnise came upstairs with his food and he sat there and ate it while trying to figure out his next move. Nice had already told him about Detective Harris and Ed meeting once a month. Now it was time to confront the detective about the situation. He just hoped Ed didn't plant a negative seed in his head because they had shot his crib up tonight.

"Baby is everything okay? You look like you are stressed out. Maybe I can do something to relieve all that tension," Yahnise said massaging his shoulders.

"You sure can little mama," EJ said pulling her around so that she was straddling him.

He lifted her shirt up and started sucking on her titties while he gripped her ass through her sweatpants.

"Take it easy Daddy," she said as he gently undressed her and laid her down on the bed and started to make love to her. They made love for hours.

CHAPTER 16

Valuable Information

Detective Harris was in his Chief's office getting a lecture on the high increase of homicides over the last month and a half.

"Something has to be done, right fucking now! I'm sick and tired of all of these bodies turning up! The Mayor is talking about bringing in the National Guard to shut shit down! Do you know what the fuck that means?" the Chief asked all of the homicide detectives within the room.

When nobody said anything, he continued. "It means they will order us around because they will have jurisdiction over us. It also means that Philadelphia will be declared in a state of emergency. Well, I'm not going to sit around and let that happen. So since the pressure is coming down from up top, I'm going to bring it down on you! I want everybody out trying to crack these cases. I'm authorizing all the overtime you need as long as I get results. If anybody fucks up, they will be writing speeding tickets for the rest of their career in law enforcement. Now get the fuck out of my office, and catch me some suspects," he said typing on his computer like no one was there.

When they all walked out of the office, another detective stopped Detective Harris. "Hey John, I need to show you something real quick," he said walking towards his desk.

"What is it Chuck, because I have to get out of here," Detective Harris said.

"It's about these homicides going on around here."

That statement caught Detective Harris' attention. "What about them?" he questioned.

"Well it seems that the feds are already on it. They are the ones that is letting this war go down. They have someone undercover within. It's a guy in the Eric Johnson organization. I suggest that you and everybody else that tries to crack this shit be careful. You know they don't like to be interfered with," the detective said.

"Who is the agent in charge of this operation?" Detective Harris asked.

The young detective looked through some paperwork on his desk. When he found the piece of paper that he was looking for, he showed Detective Harris.

Detective Harris looked at the name and smiled. "I'll be damn! My old friend gets a promotion, while I'm stuck doing homicide. I guess I will have to give you a call, Agent Kaplin," he said out loud to no one in particular.

"Thank you detective. Now don't show this information to anyone else just yet. I have to talk to a friend of mines in the bureau first. I will let you know when it's safe to let the Chief in on it. Do I have your cooperation?" Detective Harris asked giving him an evil eye.

Scared because he knew what type of person Detective Harris was and he didn't want any trouble because he had only been a detective for two months, he agreed. "Yes, you can count on me Sir," the detective said as Detective Harris walked away with a smirk on his face.

Detective Harris jumped in his car to head over to the Federal Building. He wanted to find out what the hell Agent Kaplin had EJ on his radar for this time. Most importantly, he wanted to make sure that he wasn't on any of their surveillances beings though he had been collecting money from his as payment.

***

Agent Kaplin was at the lunch truck getting a meatball sandwich when Detective Harris pulled up and parked in the official personal only parking spot. He seen him getting out of the car and waived him over.

"Hey stranger, what brings you to this neck of the woods?" Agent Kaplin asked as they walked over to a bench to talk.

"Well, I'm here on business. It was brought to my attention that you're back on the trail of Eric Johnson. What about his little shit head partner?" he asked making it seem like he didn't give a shit about either.

"Well since we did work together until that bullshit you did, I guess I can tell you."

Detective Harris smirked a little waiting for him to continue.

"Ever since Eric came home, he linked up with this big time dope connect by the name of Pedro Martinez. They are buying heroin off of him and selling it with the name, "Numbers" on it. This is some deadly shit and it has already claimed over twenty lives and counting. They meet up once or twice a month over in Delaware at a hotel called The West Inn. By the time we put a team on him, he had switched up on us. Now he has someone else meeting up with Pedro. Then on top of that, we never see him and that person together. It's almost as if they know we are watching them. I have faith that we will finally get him though, and this time every fucking charge will stick," Agent Kaplin said taking a bite of his sandwich.

Detective Harris was trying to pry a little deeper. He was searching for something helpful so he asked, "How did you come across that information? You know he keeps a tight circle and I don't see any of them folding."

"My friend that was the easy part. We have planted an agent inside that was able to give us what little bit we have right now. Our agent can get deeper than anyone else that we had. We are waiting for some reports that will give us all we need to nail these bastards once and for all," he said.

"So are you allowed to tell me who this person is? You know I still regret that mistake, and I wish I could take it back and do things the right way, but I can't. What I can do is make sure nothing gets in your way again," Detective Harris said.

"Well I still do respect you, so I guess I can tell you. You cannot say anything to anybody though because it will blow the agent's cover and if that happens, our agent will be in great danger," Agent Kaplin said.

"My lips are sealed," Detective Harris said as they walked towards the Federal Building doors.

"The name of the Agent that we have undercover is ---" Agent Kaplin said as the door closed behind him.

***

Mel and Sheed had just got finished dropping off the North Philly work. They had to go pass the houses in West Philly also to pick up some money. They had no idea that they were being followed.

When they got to 33rd and Ridge Avenue, they stopped at the little gas station on the corner to fill up before cutting through the park.

"Yo, grab a Dutch and a Pepsi while you're in there. Oh yeah, bring me a pack of Newport's too," Mel said as Sheed went to pay for the gas.

While Sheed was in the store, the male and female in the other car was putting their hoodies on, tying them tight so it would be hard to see their faces. They waited for Sheed to come out the store before they jumped out the car and started firing.

POP!

POP!

POP!

BOC!

BOC!

BOC!

BOC!

BOC!

Neither one of the two guys saw it coming until it was too late. The man hit Mel in the chest twice and once in the leg. The woman hit Sheed in the back twice and once in the head while the last two bullets went into the store's glass scaring the clerk.

The man ran and grabbed the bookbag out of the car with all of the work and money in it. After grabbing the bag, the unidentified male and female ran back to the car leaving two dead bodies laid out on the ground.

***

"Anybody heard from Mel and Sheed? They were supposed to be back two hours ago," Scrap said.

"Naw, but that's kind of weird because they are usually back as soon as they drop and pick up. We need to make some calls and see if anyone knows their whereabouts," Loud Pack said taking his phone out to make some calls.

"You do that while I give EJ a call, just in case these niggas is in some kind of trouble," Scrap said dialing EJ's number.

EJ was over at the club with Yahnise and Nyia. They were in the office going over this week's payroll. Nyia and Yahnise were the ones doing all the work while EJ was playing with Ziaire. He was waiting for them to finish so that they could head on home.

EJ's phone started ringing. He saw who it was an answered it before it went to voicemail. "Yo, what's up?"

"We have a problem. Mel and Sheed are missing in action (MIA). We've been trying to reach them ever since eight. I didn't want to disturb you, but I think something is up. That's why I waited two hours before I hit you up," Scrap said.

"Where's Chris at?" EJ wanted to know because that's who they should have been calling instead of him.

"He's on his way here now. He told me to give you a heads up," Scrap said.

"Okay, I will be there as soon as I can. Tell Chris that if anything seems fishy, to hit my cell ASAP. I want you to get a couple of niggas together and go check the North Philly spot and tell Loud Pack to go check the West Philly spot. They must have gotten into something between the two of them. I hope these nut ass pigs didn't snatch them up. Let me go so I can call my source," EJ said hanging up.

He stopped playing with Ziaire and walked out the office while making his call.

"I was just about to call you. I have some information for you," Detective Harris said trying to hold back the excitement.

"That shit can wait. Two of my Lieutenants are missing, and haven't anybody heard from them. I thought you said you would keep these assholes off of our heels. What the fuck am I paying you for?" EJ said enraged.

"I don't know who the fuck you talking to, but you better bring that shit down some. I didn't hear about anybody being picked up. I did hear that two people were shot and killed over on 33rd and Ridge. I'll see what I can find out after I stop and grab something from a friend," Detective Harris said.

EJ was tired of his bullshit. He already knew whom he was going to see because Nice had been following his backstabbing ass. He was tired of him and he was going to put a stop to it soon.

"Well, hit me when you find out."

"I have something to tell you about the company you are keeping," Detective Harris said.

"Look, I don't care about none of that shit right now. Just find my fucking workers if you want to get paid," EJ said and then hung up in his ear.

"That pussy is going to make me hurt him. Matter of fact, I think I'll let him find out the hard way who he has working for him," Detective Harris said to himself while smiling.

***

It didn't take EJ long to find out what had happened to his workers. As two of his men came out of the park on 33rd Street, they saw Mel and Sheed's car at the gas station with yellow tape around it. It was a crime scene and it was about twenty cops out there. They left the scene before anybody noticed them.

EJ knew shit was going too far now. He couldn't make any money without worrying if Ed would stick his workers up. He had heard through the grapevine that Ed was snorting Coke real bad, and even smoking Wet. That right there alone would make you do some crazy shit.

Then he thought about how in the hell did he get to two of his best shooters. They were trained in the Military Academy by some of the best Special Ops Soldiers, and now look at them.

So much shit was going on right now that EJ was wondering whom he could trust and who he could count on to have his back now. It was starting to look like anyone could be touched in these streets. He needed to go away for a few days and take a little vacation, just him, his wife, and his son.

When he got home, EJ told Yahnise to call the travel agent and book them a flight to St. Thomas for tomorrow. He was going to stay out there for about a week so he could clear his head.

The only problem was that EJ knew when he came back that he would be back to reality. He also knew that niggas better watch out because they had just reactivated a stone cold killer. *"Like you said my friend, it's going to be you or me,"* he said to himself in the mirror.

CHAPTER 17

Fleeing Apprehension

Sonja was sitting in the house talking to her friend on the phone. EJ, Yahnise, and Ziaire had already left for St. Thomas at 6:00 this morning. They told her to have a little fun while they were gone so that's what she intended to do.

"I'm glad we finally took care of that last night. I'm trying to go out today and see what else we can do," Sonja said.

"So do you want me to come and get you or will you meet me at the spot?" the man asked sitting in his car.

"I'll meet you there. We can't have anybody seeing you pick me up. We don't know who's watching us while their gone, so let's not fuck up now. I'll see you in an hour."

"Okay, see you then," the man said before hanging up.

Sonja was about to go take a shower when she decided to enter EJ and Yahnise's room. She started looking around the room as if she was making sure no one was there. She walked over and laid on their bed, smelling the clean sheets and comforter. As she laid there, she thought about how this could be *her* bed and *her* house. She removed her pajama pants and started playing with herself while looking at a picture on the nightstand of EJ, Yahnise, and Ziaire. After a few minutes, she released her juices all over their sheets.

Sonja quickly got up, leaving her cum on the bed and went to take a shower so that she could meet her partner. The whole time she was in the shower, she thought about all the ways that she was betraying her friend. *"I'm so sorry Yahnise,"* she said to herself.

***

"Let me get up out of here so I can go catch up with Scrap," Loud Pack said as he walked towards the front door.

He was over on third and Harrison, in Delaware. He had just dropped off some work to Dep and a couple of other spots. As he exited the house, he noticed a bunch of his friends playing football in the street while loud music played from a car that was double-parked. You would have thought it was summertime the way the streets were jumping, but it was only April. Loud Pack was about to get in his car when he noticed a black Charger creeping down the street at a slow pace.

His street instincts kicked in as he dove in his car and ducked down. At the same time, the passenger of the car hung halfway out the window and started unloading her semi-automatic pistol on the car that Loud Pack had just jumped in.

BOC!

BOC!

BOC!

BOC!

BOC!

BOC!

Loud Pack crawled out the other side of the car while gripping his 9mm. When he reached the ground, he quickly sprung up and started firing at the car as it bent the corner. People were scattering all over the place. Loud Pack jumped in his bullet-riddled car and pulled off before the cops showed up.

He was driving down Route 95 ten minutes later, trying to make it back to Philly without getting pulled over. As he was getting close to the Philadelphia Pike exit, a state trooper jumped in the back of him and hit the sirens.

"FUCK! FUCK! FUCK!" was all Loud Pack could say. He was contemplating trying to run, but he thought about it and decided that it might not be the best idea. He knew one thing for sure, and that was he wasn't going to no Howard R Young Correctional Facility. He pulled over and pulled out his 9mm making sure that it was cocked and loaded.

The office sat in his car for a few minutes before opening up his car door, stepping out, and putting his hat on.

Loud Pack didn't want to let him get close to the car because then he would see that the windows had been shot out and there were bullet holes on the side.

As soon as he got close enough to the car, Loud Pack opened the door and jumped out gripping his nine. The Trooper tried to reach for his weapon, but it was too late.

BOC!

BOC!

Lout Pack hit the Trooper in his right shoulder and right leg so he couldn't pull his gun out.

The Trooper fell to the ground as Loud Pack ran up on him putting two shots in the Trooper's torso and one in his face.

BOC!

BOC!

BOC!

He saw that the Trooper wasn't moving so he ran and jumped back in his car leaving the Trooper on the side of the road to die. As he drove down the highway, he kept checking his mirrors making sure he wasn't being followed. He got off at the airport exit and took the long way home trying to avoid any traffic and cop cars. He had just survived a hit on his life and the possibility of being arrested by killing a cop. Little did he know, the Trooper's cruiser camera was on and had recorded the whole thing.

***

Shannon and Tiffany had just returned from Seattle while on a business trip. They had invested their money into something that would or could possibly make them millions. They were the co-founders of an internet marketing company specializing in website design and pay per click advertising.

Tiffany wanted to do something legit with all of the money she had so she had talked Shannon into backing her up. When they went out to Seattle to see the marketing team, it was a wrap. They were sold on the project and they did all of the proper signing and ironed out all of the technicalities in one day. Now that they were back, it was time to make sure shit was straight for EJ.

He had asked them to keep an eye on things while he was gone. He had told them that Chris was running the show, but if he needed help with anything, to just intervene and give him a hand. They both knew they wouldn't have to do too much, but they also knew to be ready for anything.

They headed over to Millick Street first. Since that was the base for their operation, they decided to see how it was going.

When they pulled up to 60th and Market, Shannon noticed that Detective Harris was talking to Ed inside of the car in the front of them. They didn't even notice the two beautiful women in the car in the back of them because they were so deep in their own conversation.

"Let's follow them and see what they are up to," Tiff said to Shannon while cruising at a safe distance behind them.

They followed them for ten minutes until they pulled up to a Crown Victoria that was parked on 60th and Haverford. Detective Harris got out of the car and Ed handed him a book bag.

"Do you see what I see?" Tiff asked.

"Hell yeah, that's one of the bags that we use when we are picking up or dropping off. I knew that nigga was really against us. He probably was the one helping Ed rob all the spots," Shannon said pissed off.

"Let's get out of here. We're not going to bother EJ while he is on vacation, but as soon as he returns, it's on and popping," Tiff said.

***

The death of the Delaware State Trooper was all over the news and Loud Pack's face was posted as the number one suspect. He didn't know that when an officer turns on his flashers, it also activates the dash cam. Now he had every law enforcement agency in the tristate area and more looking for him. Actually, it was a one hundred thousand dollar reward out for him already, which meant anybody was capable of turning him in.

Loud Pack was hiding out at one of the stash spots in West Philly because his house had already been raided by US Marshalls and the Feds. He needed to get far away as possible from all this drama. He called Scrap and told him everything that had went down. Scrap told him to lay low until he got there with his going away money.

They both already knew that every train, bus, and airport would be under tight surveillance, so they decided to get him out of town by car.

Scrap pulled up in front of the house, in an all-black Tahoe with twenty-five percent tint on the windows. The tint was the legal percentage so he wouldn't attract unwanted attention. Scrap had one of his female workers follow him in his Bentley. She was going to be the one to drive him far away from here. That way when they pulled up at a toll or had to get gas, she would be the one handling it.

Loud Pack came out of the house with his baseball cap on covering his face. He jumped in the truck with Scrap so they could talk.

"Damn, Dawg! Do you know every fucking cop in the city is looking for you?" Scrap said to Loud Pack.

"Yeah man, I wish I would have just seen what he wanted first instead of getting all paranoid and shit," Loud Pack said.

"Well, it's half a million in those book bags. Tara will be your driver and she will take you as far away from here as possible. I gave her fifty thousand dollars to make sure she drops you off at a safe place. Once you are safe, she will come back and you will be on your own. When you get to your destination, buy a prepaid phone, and hit me up. Once this shit boils over, then maybe you will be able to come back. This is for your protection because if those pigs catch you now, they will definitely kill you," Scrap said handing Loud Pack a gun.

Loud Pack knew that they would shoot first and ask questions later. "I appreciate this man. Does EJ know about this shit yet?"

"I didn't want to bother him while he was spending quality time with his family in the sun. Chris said when he talked to him; he would give him an update."

"Well I guess I should be going then. Tell Tara I'm ready to get up out of here before somebody sees me and decides to play hero," Loud Pack said.

They shook hands and gave each other a half hug before Scrap exited the vehicle. Tara came and jumped in the driver's seat. "What's up nigga? Your ass stay getting into shit. Roll this shit up. We might as well get fucked up on our way," she said as she plugged her phone into the Bose system and hit play on her playlist. Kendrick Lamar blasted through the system as they headed for the highway.

CHAPTER 18

Refreshed

When EJ and his family returned from their vacation, he felt refreshed and energized. As they walked in the door, Sonja greeted them with a hug. "Hey y'all! How was the trip?"

"Girl, we had the best time ever. Come on, I'll tell you all about it while you help me unpack," Yahnise said as they went upstairs.

EJ headed downstairs to look at some work he had neglected to do while he was gone. Before he started looking at the paperwork, he decided to see what was going on at his house while he was gone. He went over to the computer and typed a password in. Instantly, four small screens popped up showing different areas of the house.

He started off by going back to the day that they left. When he saw Sonja get into their bedroom, be brought the screen up full mode. He watched as she went over to the bed and laid on it. He then watched her pull off her pajama pants and start playing with herself. After she finished, she left out of their room.

"Damn, this girl is fucking crazy," EJ said to himself. He watched every day that they were gone, and just like the first day, she went in their room and masturbated on their bed. EJ was sick, but he knew that it was his entire fault for getting involved with another woman, especially his wife's best friend. He only did it to get back at her for trying to play him back when they were all in high school.

After he finished watching the video, he turned the computer off and did the paperwork that was waiting for him.

EJ forgot to turn his phone on when they left the airport. He had it off the whole time they were gone. That way, nobody could disturb them while they enjoyed the beach. As soon as he turned it back on, he seen that he had over thirty text messages and voicemails.

While he was going through them, his phone started ringing. "I was just reading the message. What happened?" he asked Scrap.

Scrap ran the whole chain of events down to him while EJ listened to his every word.

"Damn, so he's cool now, right? He needs to stay away for a while, because if those pigs catch him, they are going to give him the death penalty with no judge," EJ said after Scrap filled him in.

"So what do you want to do about Detective Harris?" Scrap asked after he told him what Tiff and Shannon had saw.

"I'm going to deal with his ass tomorrow. I don't know if he's trying to set me up or not, now. I have let his sneaking around with the enemy go on for too long. Tomorrow night, we will pay him a visit. I'm about to go cook dinner for my family so I'll hit you up later."

"Go ahead with your soft ass. I always knew Yahnise wore the pants in that mutha-fucka!" Scrap said laughing.

EJ hung up on him smirking as he went upstairs to the kitchen.

***

Two hours later, they were all sitting at the table eating the delicious dinner that EJ had made. He had put together some scrumptious beef teriyaki and rice with a tray of jumbo shrimp and cocktail sauce on the side. Yahnise and Sonja were sipping on a chilled glass of Moscoto, while EJ was enjoying a cold Pepsi. Ziaire was in his highchair eating his food while the adults sat around the table laughing and talking about nothing in particular.

"I want to thank the both of you for allowing me to stay here longer than I expected. I know I said I would be out of here in a couple of weeks, but I'm still here and it's been over a couple of months. It's just feels so good being here," Sonja said changing the subject.

"Girl, we don't mind. You're like family and family always looks out for each other," Yahnise said grabbing Sonja's hand.

"Yeah, you can stay until you are ready to go," EJ said giving Sonja a crazy look. He was still thinking about the video and how she was playing with her pussy on their mattress.

"I appreciate the both of you and if it's anything I can do to show my gratitude, please just let me know," she said staring at EJ without Yahnise noticing.

EJ got up to clear the table because he knew his wife was about to leave to go to the club.

"Let me get out of here. Are you going out tonight or staying in?" Yahnise asked EJ.

"I think me and little man are going to enjoy some cartoons tonight. Ain't that right Zi?" EJ said to his son.

Ziaire was happy that he was staying with his dad. He didn't care what they did, as long as he was with him.

"What's your plans for tonight, Sonja?" Yahnise asked as she grabbed her car keys and cellphone.

"I'm just going to clean up the dishes and maybe watch your two big head boys tear shit up around here," she said as they both laughed.

"Okay, I'll see y'all when I get home. Don't worry baby, if I need you, I'll call you," she said giving EJ and Zi a kiss before heading out the door.

EJ and Zi went into the living room and started watching TV. Sonja stayed in the kitchen and cleaned up after the fabulous meal that EJ had cooked for all of them. She had something to take care of tonight, but she put it off hoping to score with EJ one last time.

***

It was after 10:00 p.m. Ziaire was in his room sleeping after watching a couple of hours of cartoons with his dad. EJ was in his bedroom laying down enjoying some down time when Sonja knocked on the door. She opened the door and came right in after she knocked two times.

"Are you busy?"

"Naw, just watching a movie," he said.

"What is it?" she asked walking over towards the bed. She had on some sweatpants and a wife beater.

"About Last Night with Regina Hall and Kevin Hart," he said.

"Oh shit! That's my favorite movie. That nigga is a clown in that."

"Yeah, he is a funny mutha-fucka. You can sit down and watch it with me if you want to," he said.

"Why not," she said as she got in the bed next to EJ.

They watched the movie in silence for a while. They were laughing at a part when Sonja slid a little closer to EJ and put her hand on his chest. EJ sat up straight, moved her hand, and looked at her.

"I have a question for you. Why did you come in here while we were gone and masturbate on my sheets?"

That question caught her off guard. She wondered how the hell he even knew she had done that. "What y'all on some freaky shit? Where are the cameras at?" she asked.

"Right there," EJ said pointing to the webcam on the computer. He didn't want to tell her about the hidden cameras that were installed everywhere else to protect his house. Only he and Yahnise knew about them.

"Damn, I guess I'm busted, huh? I've been a bad girl so you need to give me a spanking," she said standing up on the bed and pulling her sweatpants off.

She had on a red-laced thong. He pussy lips looked like they were swollen the way they were trying to get free. EJ just watched her, as she took off her tank top and then her thong. Now she was standing on his bed completely naked.

"I can't do this shit anymore," he said as he tried to cover her up with a blanket.

She sat right on his lap. She could tell that he was lying because his dick was busting through his sweatpants. "Are you sure that you don't want to do this anymore?" she said grinding on his dick.

He pushed her off of him and got up off of the bed. His dick was hard as a rock right now and she could see it. "You need to get the fuck out of my room right now. I told you that we can't do this shit no more. What do you think my wife would have said if she had seen you playing with yourself on her bed? Did you ever stop to think about that? Did you?" he barked at her causing her to jump a little.

"Tomorrow, I'm going to talk to some real-estate people that I know and try to get you a crib of your own. I'll pay the first year's mortgage and then the rest will be on you," EJ said angrily.

"What the fuck is that supposed to be; hush money? I don't need no handouts from you. I thought you were starting to come around. When we were in high school, you and your friend used to wish that you could sit in the same room as us, let alone touch this pussy. Now all of a sudden, you don't want none of this," Sonja said rubbing up and down her body.

"You are crazy. Can you please go," EJ said not trying to hear anymore of her foolishness.

Sonja grabbed her clothes and left out of the bedroom slamming the door behind her. When she walked to her room, she started smiling as if nothing had ever happened. She already knew they had hidden cameras in the house, she just didn't know where.

"Pretty soon, you won't be smiling anymore. I can't wait to see your face when your life is over and nobody can come to your rescue this time," she said as she laid on her bed and drifted off to sleep.

***

The next morning EJ woke up to the smell of bacon, eggs, and home fries. When he came downstairs, Yahnise was in the kitchen setting the table. EJ walked up behind her and grabbed her putting his arms around her waist. "Mmmmmm, I love when I'm greeted like this. Is that a flashlight, or are you just happy to see me?" she asked pushing her ass back on his dick.

"Let's find out," he said lifting her skirt and pulling out his dick. He took one hand and moved her panties to the side while guiding his dick inside her walls with his other hand.

Yahnise gasped as she bent over the table and started throwing it back on him. After a few minute, they both came simultaneously. She fixed her skirt while he fixed his pants. "Damn, that was the best quickie I have ever had. Now I have to go wash up again before I go pick up Nyia."

"Where are you two headed?"

"Me, her, and Sonja are going to talk to some real estate people today. Sonja wants to get a crib over on Beach Street and we have an appointment at eleven," Yahnise said heading for the stairs.

"That's good! If you need me to do anything to help, let me know. I'm about to go out to Philly. I have to take care of a few things."

"See you later, then. I love you," Yahnise said blowing him a kiss.

"Love you too," EJ said grabbing his keys and heading out the door.

***

EJ pulled up to Chris' car dealership to pick up his new car. Chris had ordered him a 2014 red Aston Martin DB9 with chrome twenty-four Asanti wheels. Chris had to get them to cut the wheel well just to fit the wheels on it. When EJ saw the car pull up from the back, he just smiled. That shit had to be the most beautiful car he had ever laid eyes on. He jumped in and told Chris to come on.

"I have to stay here until my new shipment comes. I will meet you at the crib later."

"Thanks again," EJ said as he peeled off bumping MMG through the ten thousand dollar sound system.

All eyes were on his wheels as he drove down Market Street on his way to the jewelry store across from the Gallery. Women stared as their panties got wet just from looking at his hot new ride. He parked right in the front of the store so that everybody could see him step out.

As he walked in the jewelry store, Kyle said, "Damn nigga! I don't think anybody will be able to top that shit!"

"That's why I did it. Now is my watch ready; so I can really shit on these niggas?"

"Yeah, it's right here," Kyle said pulling out the Yacht Master Tri billion cut Rolex with red diamonds all around it.

"Got Damn! That shit is sick," EJ said putting it on. "Thanks man for getting this shit for me on time. I have to go see some people, but come pass the club tonight. I have something for you.

"I'll see you later, my nigga," Kyle said giving his friend a pound.

When EJ walked out the door, a parking meter lady was trying to give him a ticket. "Whoa! Whoa! Here I go right here, baby!"

When she turned around, she smiled at him. "I know this is not your bomb ass car," Lisa said seductively.

Lisa and EJ go way back. He used to fuck with her when he was in high school. They met up a while ago when he seen her on his old block out Southwest. That was the place where he used to do the checks and other money laundering shit. He hadn't seen her since he had been home.

"Yeah, this is me baby girl. How have you been?"

"I'm good. You see where I work now. I got tired of being in these streets doing dumb shit. I have my own crib now on 59th and Lansdowne. You should come see me sometime. We can talk for a while or something," she said trying to give him a hint that she wanted to fuck his rich ass.

"We'll see. Put your number in my phone and I'll hit you up later," EJ said passing her his phone. As she was putting her number in, EJ noticed all of the girls at the bus stop staring at him and his car. All he had to do was wave them over and they would have hauled ass over to him.

"Make sure you use it, this time," Lisa said giving him a hug in front of all of the jealous girls watching.

"Don't worry, I will," EJ said as he jumped in his car and peeled of leaving a lot of women just staring at him.

CHAPTER 19

Slipping

Tara and Loud Pack were out in Walnut Creek California. They had been driving for days, only stopping to switch drivers, eat, get gas, or use the restroom.

"Let's find a hotel around here. It should be cool. I really don't think anybody will know who I am this far out," Loud Pack said.

"Good, because a bitch needs to take a shower. Once I do that, I'll take a nap before jumping on a plane back to Philly," Tara said pulling into a Days Inn.

"This ain't no damn hotel! Why are you stopping here?"

"Nigga, you don't need to be in a hotel! You need to be low key until shit cools down! Now man the fuck up and chill while I get you a fucking room!" Tara snapped.

Loud Pack looked at her with lust in his eyes as she walked into the office to get a room. Tara wasn't your average hood rat. She was a rider from Southwest and she was a go-getter. If you got into something, she would help you shoot your way out of it.

"Damn, that's one crazy bitch right there," Loud Pack thought as he waited for her to come out.

A few minutes later, Tara came back out with the room key. She hopped back in the Tahoe and passed it to him. She drove around the corner and all the way to the end of the building. "This is it, right here. I'm going to chill here until tomorrow morning. When I wake up, I'm going to take a cab to LAX. Now bring that Loud out the glove compartment with you," she said getting out and grabbing her bag.

Loud Pack grabbed his shit, and the Loud, and went inside. The room was very big and it only had a couch, a queen sized bed, a refrigerator, and a fifty-two inch plasma TV in it.

"Well it looks like this will be my home for a while," Loud Pack said sitting on the bed.

"It's paid up for six months so you don't have to pay these people shit out of your own pocket. That was from your peoples, cause we look out for each other. I'll be right back; I'm going to take a shower. You can have your bed. I'll sleep on the couch tonight. By tomorrow night, I should be back on the East Coast," Tara said heading for the bathroom.

Loud Pack sat down and rolled up while Tara was in the shower. He was thinking about how his life had come to this. He was getting money, fucking bad bitches, driving hot cars, and now he was on the fucking run.

After he finished rolling up, he turned the TV on. He started watching the NBA playoffs. The LA Clippers were playing Golden State. Tara came out of the bathroom wearing a pair of Baby Phat shorts. As she walked pass the TV, her ass was jiggling. From the looks of it, Loud Pack could tell that she wasn't wearing any panties and if she was, they were thongs.

"Spark that shit up," Tara said drying her hair.

The two of them sat and smoked until one in the morning before they laid down to go to sleep. "You don't have to lay on that couch. It's plenty of room on this bed. I won't touch you, if that's what you are thinking," Loud Pack said.

"I'm not worried about you touching me, nigga. It's the other way around. I might hurt your ass," she said laughing.

She came over and jumped in the bed with her back to Loud Pack. He turned the TV off and just laid there in the dark.

"What you scared to get close to me? Let me find out your ass is scared of pussy," Tara said.

"I'm not scared of shit, but going to jail for the rest of my life," Loud Pack shot back.

"Well, prove it nigga," she said pulling off her shorts and opening her legs up so Loud Pack could see her pussy.

He wasted no time giving her what they both needed so badly. They sexed each other until 6:00 a.m. Their sex session only ended then because Tara had to get to the airport before 8:00 so she wouldn't miss her 9:00 flight.

When the plane was in the air, Tara used the air phone to call Scrap and inform him that she was in route back. After she hung up, she leaned back and dozed off until her flight was over.

***

EJ had held off on dealing with Detective Harris for trying to play both sides of the field. It was bad enough that he was bribing him, but to be dealing with his enemy also was just too much. He decided to wait until they met up for the payment to address this little issue.

That time had finally came. EJ told him that he was going to meet him at his house. Detective Harris was against that at first because his wife was there, but when she called telling him that she had some errands to run, he decided to do it.

When Detective Harris pulled up to his house, EJ and Scrap were waiting outside on his porch. He didn't really think too much of it, so he got out of his car and invited them in.

"How the hell did y'all beat me here?" he asked taking his jacket off, but leaving his gun in the holster.

"We were already in the area so when you gave us the address, we came straight here," EJ said to ease his suspicions.

"Oh, okay. Do you have my money?" he said getting straight to the point.

"Yeah we have it, but I have a question or two for you first," EJ said. At the same time, Scrap pulled out his gun aiming it at Detective Harris.

"What the hell are you doing?" Detective Harris asked as EJ took his gun from him and then reached down and pulled his ankle holster off also that contained his throw away gun.

"Like I said before, I have a couple of questions for you. Answer them truthfully and we won't have any problems. If you lie to me, then well you already know what the consequences will be. Now sit the fuck down in that chair," EJ said pointing a chair at the kitchen table.

Once Detective Harris was seated, Scrap took both sets of handcuffs and cuffed him to the chair. Then he took the duct tape and wrapped it around his whole body.

EJ pulled up a chair, sitting in front of Detective Harris. "Now what I want to know is what have you been talking to Ed about?"

"I don't know what the hell you are talking about. I do business with you and you only, man, I swear," Detective Harris said.

"So you are gonna sit here and tell me that you haven't been meeting with Ed at secret locations and receiving payments from him."

"No man! I put that on my family that I wouldn't do no shit like that. I was waiting for you to give me the word and I would have taken care of him for you," he said trying to get himself off of the hook.

"See that's where we have a problem at. How do I know you haven't told him the same shit you are telling me? You are a very good liar, I'll give you that," EJ said standing up.

"I swear on everything that I love, I have never tried to set you up, man."

"You keep saying that. Do you really put that on your family's lives?" EJ asked him to make sure he heard him right.

"Nigga, I don't have to fucking like to you or any fucking body else. Like I said, I haven't talked to no fucking Ed. Now take this shit off of me and let me go and I won't put your little follower in a jail cell," he said growing some balls.

"Okay, if this is how you want to play. Scrap, you know what to do," EJ said shaking his head.

Scrap walked away leaving the room. "I thought you would have been a much smarter man. I paid you well to look out for my crew. Instead, you tip my enemy off so that he could rob my houses. Now that you were caught riding around with him, you still playing dumb," EJ said looking at him.

Detective Harris was stunned by what EJ had just said. *"How does he know that I was with him? Did somebody see me?"* he thought to himself.

Before he got the chance to say anything, Scrap walked back in the room with two other people. Detective Harris looked and saw his wife and son. His heart started beating fast as he saw them sit in the other two chairs.

EJ stood up and looked at the detective. "See, I have you every opportunity to tell me the truth. I even gave you a chance to take back that statement about your family, but your ignorance has become their downfall. You said you put it on your family's lives and you lied so I guess that's their lives then," EJ said and nodded to Scrap.

"PLEASE NOOOOOOOOO! DON'T DO THIS!" was all his wife was able to say before two shots caught her in the heart.

PHHH!

PHHH!

Her body fell out of the chair and hit the floor. Their son started crying for his mom before he joined her.

PHHH!

PHHH!

PHHH!

The shots ripped through the sixteen year olds body like a knife cutting through hot butter just before he fell on the floor beside his mom.

"What the fuck have you done? I'm going to kill you bastards! I'll see you both in hell!" Detective Harris said.

"Don't you mean, what have *you* done? You are the one who betrayed me and put your lie on your family, but on another note, I'll see you when I get there. Keep my bed warm for me you fucking pig!" EJ said pulling out his 40 caliber putting two shots in Detective Harris' head.

BLOC!

BLOC!

He turned to Scrap, "Did you find the money that his wife said was in the bedroom?"

"Yeah, it's over by the door. Let's get out of here before the cleanup crew gets here. I already called them before I went to get his wife and kid," Scrap said as they headed out the door.

"Did you tell them to make sure that it looks like a robbery gone bad?" EJ asked as they hopped in the car.

Scrap nodded his head yes, as they drove back to the house on Millick Street so EJ could get his car.

***

Loud Pack was sitting in the hotel room bored to death. He wasn't used to sitting around like this. It had been a week since he had went anywhere so he decided to go down the street to the Nordstrom department store.

He grabbed his keys, took ten thousand dollars out of his bag, and headed out the door. When he got in the truck, he had forget that he had left his cell phone in his room. He ran back inside the room, grabbed his phone, and left for the mall.

Loud Pack always wore a fitted cap when he went to the mall. Today he decided he was only going to wear sunglasses. Once he picked out a couple of items, he headed for the cashier counter.

He saw this bad ass looking red bone wearing hardly anything. She had on a skimpy ass pair of shorts, a sports bra, and a pair of sandals. She was in line waiting to pay for her stuff. "Let me take care of that for you, Ma," Loud Pack said as they reached the counter.

"Thanks, but no thanks," she said not even turning around.

Loud Pack stared at her for a minute before saying, "It's no problem beautiful, it's the least I can do."

"I said no thanks, plus my man wouldn't approve," the lady said pulling out her money to pay for her items.

"Fuck your man and fuck you too then with your stuck up ass! I was just trying to be generous," Loud Pack said moving to the next cashier that was ready.

"Yeah, that's why you are mad, because I wouldn't let you fuck me. You are a dumb ass nigga. I'll make sure I let my man know that you were in here disrespecting me and him."

"Tell him what the fuck you want to tell him. As a matter of fact, tell him I said eat a dick and die," he said grabbing his dick for emphasis.

"We'll see about that," she said talking on her cell phone while walking out of the store.

A few minutes later, Loud Pack was walking out of the store when he saw the red bone chick standing with some skinny nigga wearing a tank top. He laughed at the thought of this frail ass nigga trying to come at him. He walked out the door ready for whatever.

As soon as he was outside, all he heard was, "FREEZE! US MARSHALS! GET ON THE GROUND NOW!"

Around ten agents swarmed on him including the red bone and the skinny nigga. They were both US Marshalls just waiting for him to come out. Loud Pack didn't even know how the hell they had found him. All he did know was, he was about to go to jail for a very long time.

They had been watching him for two days now. When he was in the mall a week ago, a lady had recognized him from the wanted alert that came up on her phone. She immediately notified the FBI's Fugitive Task Force. They were just waiting for confirmation so they sent one of their agents down in undercover because who could turn down a fine looking woman in sexy clothes. Loud Pack fell for the bait, but what he didn't know was she was wearing a camera inside of her earrings that sent his face to a computer for facial recognition. Once they received a positive ID on him, they waited for him to come out of the store so they could arrest him.

"We've been looking for you, Mr. Donnie Stevens. What did you think; that if you came to the West Coast that no one would know who you were? You're a cop killer so there is no place to run or hide, my friend," the agent said putting him in a tinted out Crown Victoria.

He still had all of his money sitting in the hotel room. He didn't even get a chance to spend twenty grand of the money yet. *"Whoever cleans that room is about to be a rich ass mutha-fucka,"* he thought to himself as they took him to a federal prison where he would wait for an extradition hearing.

CHAPTER 20

Old Friend

"*I*n a robbery gone wrong, Detective John Harris, his wife Melissa Harris, and their sixteen year old son John, Jr. were shot and killed execution style. Their house was ransacked and anything of value was stolen. Police have no suspects at this time. They are going house to house to see if anybody seen anything suspicious. It is like a circus out here with FBI, Philadelphia Police, Upper Darby State Police, and a host of other jurisdictions helping with this manhunt because another one of their own has become victim to the violence. We will have more for you tonight at eleven, about the cities fifth cop killing this year. I'm Donna Reeves reporting live from West Philadelphia.*"

Ed cut the TV off with a smile on his face. "Damn, somebody got to that piece of shit before me."

"Who are you talking about baby?" the fake CoCo looking white girl said sitting on the bed butt naked after taking a shower. She and Ed had just got finished an hour long wild sex session.

"Oh nothing. I was just thinking out loud," he said playing with her nipples.

She laid back on the bed and stuck two fingers in her pussy while Ed sucked on her titties. He knew that they had to hurry up so he didn't want to waste any more time than needed.

Ed's dick was hard as a rock now, just from watching her play with herself. He got off the bed and pulled her to the edge spreading her legs wide open. When he entered her wet gushy pussy, she came instantly. "OHHHHH SHIT BABY! FUCK ME HARDER!" she screamed.

The white girl's pussy was so tight that Ed thought he was fucking a virgin. It didn't matter that they had just finished fucking for an hour; she pussy was still just as tight as the first time.

"OH MY! THAT'S IT BABY! YESSSSS! GET YOUR SHIT OFF CAUSE I'M CUMMMIN!" she screamed releasing her juices again. It was as if she came every couple of minutes.

Ed started hitting it harder and harder, opening her legs wider. Then he took his thumb and started rubbing her clit, stimulating her even more. As soon as he was about to cum, he pulled out and busted all over her stomach.

"Ummmmm," she said wiping the cum all over her body with her hand.

Ed got up, got his clothes, and started getting dressed. "Damn baby! You make a nigga never want to leave!"

"Now I have to take another shower," the girl said grabbing the mirror full of Coke off the nightstand and taking a hit.

"Let me get some of that before I go," Ed said sitting next to her, taking a line of Coke. Then he took another one before walking out the door.

Ed needed to be out of his mind for what he was about to do. He was tired of everything and he felt as though it was time to kill or be killed. He really didn't care that the city had every law enforcement in the tristate area out looking for the people or person that had killed another cop. He jumped in his car and headed out to visit an old friend.

***

EJ had just left the barbershop on 58th and Woodland and he was heading over to see Lisa. He had called her and invited her out to lunch. When he pulled up in his Aston Martin, her pussy started throbbing.

"Do you always show off like this?" she asked getting in the car. Lisa was dressed very casual with a pink tennis skirt, white Polo shirt with the pink logo, and a pair of pink and white Jordan's on. Lisa looked like a model and she had the body to accommodate everything.

"I only do it when I'm trying to impress a certain person. So where do you want to go eat at?" EJ asked.

"How about the Chinese buffet? You know that's my favorite food."

"I'm surprised you haven't turned into a shrimp and broccoli yet," EJ said smiling at her. He hit a button on the steering wheel and the sounds of Avant came out of the sound system.

♪ ♪ *Silhouettes of a perfect frame. Shadows of your smile will always remain, always remain. Beginners love, so fades away...* ♪ ♪

"No you didn't put this song on. This was our first song that we made love or should I say, had sex to. We didn't even know what we were doing," Lisa said leaning back in the seat enjoying the music.

"That was then. I know what I'm doing now," EJ said looking at her. He reached over, put his hand between her legs, and started massaging her pussy. She closed her eyes and opened her legs up even wider for him.

"Well, let's go somewhere and see what you learned then," Lisa said seductively while she enjoyed the finger massage EJ was giving her pussy.

He looked at her and licked his lips as he turned off of Gray's Gerry Avenue and headed for a motel.

Lisa thought to herself, *"I'm about to fuck the shit out of this nigga."* A smile crept across her face as she enjoyed the music and the feeling of EJ's hand.

♪ ♪ *I'll keep an old candy coated Valentine. Visions of you, when you were mine. A tarnished dream...* ♪ ♪

***

Ed found the person he was looking for. He pulled over and started watching her every move. When she came out of the daycare, Ed jumped out of the car. He walked over to her, and when she seen who it was, a smile came across her face.

"What are you doing down here?" she asked sitting her son on the top of her car.

"I came to see you. I think that it's time to put that Plan B into motion. I'm tired of playing with this nigga. He's running around like he runs the city and everybody has to bow down to him," Ed said leaning on the car.

She opened the door and put her son in the car. After she strapped her son in, she shut the door. "I've been waiting for you to come around. Your son really needs his real father in his life. I'm tired of pretending so what are you going to do?" she asked leaning in to kiss him passionately.

"You know what, after this is all over, I promise you will have my full attention. You and our son. So are you ready to kill EJ and everybody around him?" he asked looking at her.

"I'll do whatever it takes to make sure my son has his father in his life. If that means laying someone down, then so be it," she said sincerely.

They stood there talking for a few more minutes before Ed jumped in his car and left. He had the one person EJ would never expect to betray him on his team. Now it was just a matter of time before he would be able to take over EJ's drug organization.

Numbers were spreading everywhere. The whole East coast was talking about the popular drug. What made the fiends want it even more was the fact that people were dying from it. EJ had made millions off of it, while Ed was barely only making one million off of Blood Game and it was, the same product that he had stolen from EJ. Ed knew it was the name that was selling, that's why he wanted it.

Ed was on his way back to his snow bunny's crib to snort some Coke. He smiled just from thinking about what he was about to do.

***

EJ and Lisa laid in the bed at the Hyatt Hotel, sweaty from making love for the last two hours. He couldn't lie, her pussy was the bomb, and she had multiple orgasms because she was wearing a clit ring. He made a reminder to himself to try and talk Yahnise into getting one.

"Baby, you have really grew up from when we were younger," Lisa said looking at the size of his dick.

"I have to say the same about you. How did you learn how to work those pussy muscles like that? You were all the way turned up," EJ said playing in her hair as she rested her head on his chest.

"Yoga," she said laughing.

"Whatever girl! Let's get dressed so I can get you back home," he said getting up to put his clothes on.

"If you didn't have a family now, do you think it would have been a chance for us now? I know we both had our problems, but we were so young with so much life ahead of us. Shit, we are still young, but we are also much more mature than we were back then."

"I really can't answer that question because I do have a wife and son now. Even though we just did what we did, I really do love my wife and I would die for her if I ever had to," EJ said sitting on the bed putting his clothes on.

"Fair enough. Can I see you again? I'm from the hood so I know how to play my position," Lisa said smiling.

EJ grabbed her and kissed her neck. "As long as you know what this is, I don't have a problem with that."

She smiled at him, got up, and started to put her clothes on.

***

After EJ dropped Lisa off, he called his wife. "What are you doing, beautiful?"

"Nothing, I just picked Zi up and we are heading home. Why? Do you have something planned for us, Daddy?" Yahnise asked in a sexy voice.

"Yeah, as a matter of fact, I do. Let's take Zi to Chuckie Cheese so he can have some fun. Then later on tonight, I was thinking that me and you could play in the Jacuzzi and maybe have a little water fight," EJ said.

"That sounds wonderful. I guess you have yourself a date. Do you want us to meet you there or what?"

"I'll meet you at the house in about an hour. I'm going to stop pass Savino's office and drop his paperwork (money) off. After that, I will jump on the highway and head on home. That should give you a little time to freshen up," EJ said heading to Chester to meet Savino at the Harrah's so he could wash his dirty money.

When he pulled up, Savino was sitting in his 2014 Mercedes Benz S-class smoking a cigarette. EJ stepped out of his car and popped the trunk.

"This is $300,000.00. I will bring you another three hundred grand tomorrow after my people do their pickups," EJ said to Savino as he placed the bag in the backseat.

"That will be cool. I'm about to go cash in on some poker and blackjack. Check your account when you get home. It looks like you are at the forty million mark."

"That's good, but it ain't all mine. I have a team so they will be getting a nice cut of that. Well, let me get out of here Sir. My wife is waiting for me to come do the family thing. You know how that is," he said shaking Savino's hand.

"Do you baby? Just make sure you stop at the office tomorrow. I have something to show you. It's about some new investments that I think you should look into," Savino said before he pulled off.

EJ pulled off right behind him. He rode right pass the bombed out (tinted) Tahoe. The four agents had been taking pictures of him and his lawyer ever since they pulled up. Agent Kaplin was in the front passenger seat and his undercover agent was sitting in the backseat.

"I can almost guarantee that it was money in that bag that he just gave him. Now all we have to do is catch him in the act and then we can get him and that no good ass lawyer of his," Agent Kaplin said.

"Do you think he has been the one behind all of those other murders that have been taking place? I never heard him talk about them to anybody," the undercover agent asked Agent Kaplin.

"I'm sure he is, but we have to prove it first. That's why I need you to figure out a way to get it out of him. I also think that he had something to do with Detective Harris and his family getting murdered. I just have to prove that also."

"What about his ex-friend Ed? I'm thinking it could have also been him. They met up a lot at different places. He could have gotten tired of being extorted from him and knocked him off," the agent said.

"You may be right! You really just may be right! Let's get out of here. It's time to tighten up a little," Agent Kaplin said as they headed back to the headquarters.

CHAPTER 21

Block Party

It was July 4th (Independence Day), and EJ and Chis had decided to throw a big ass block party/cookout. They had blocked the whole 39th Street off from, 39th and Haverford to 39th and Brown. EJ spent a little over fifteen grand just on the food and liquor alone. Chris had spent around the same amount on entertainment such as activities for the kids, a DJ, an off duty police officer for security, etc. They didn't care about going to war with Ed, but it was too many kids outside so they wanted to protect them. At least today, everybody could enjoy themselves. EJ and Yahnise pulled up in his Aston Martin, while Chris and Nyia pulled up in a Bentley Continental drop top. Their Bentley was powder blue with cream interior. He had twenty-four inch Giovanna wheels on it and they were practically blinding people as they drove through the barricade.

They parked their cars right on Melon Street so that everybody could see how much money they were getting. Yahnise's mom had brought all of the kids there with her.

When EJ stepped out of the car, he looked like and smelled like money. He had on a red and white Prada short set with all white Prada shoes. He had on a blinged out watch and chain set made by Johnny's Custom Jeweler's. To complete his setup, he had on a pair of Prada sunglasses.

Yahnise stepped out of the car in an all-white Sam Edelmon skirt set. She had a pair of Sam Edelman Genette sandals on her feet. She was also wearing her iced out necklace and bracelet set from Tiffany's that EJ had purchased for her for their three-year anniversary.

Chris and Nyia were rocking all Polo gear and they were looking fresh. No one could take their eyes off the two couples as they walked around greeting everyone like they were hood superstars.

The smell of burgers, ribs, and hotdogs had EJ's stomach growling. He wanted something to eat because he hadn't eat anything all day.

"I'll be back in a few minutes. I'm going to grab some food. Do you want anything while I'm gone?" he asked his wife.

"Just bring me something to drink, please," she said giving him a kiss.

EJ headed over to the table with all of the food on it. As he made his way through the crowd, he spotted Shannon and Tiffany. He walked over to them and grabbed them by their waist.

"Hey you two beautiful ladies. Why are you standing here alone?"

Tiffany hugged him and said, "Because you didn't cum in my mouth in a while. I still crave for it, sometimes. You know how we do. What happens behind closed doors stays behind closed doors."

EJ was smiling at her because he didn't know what to say. She had left him speechless. He gave Shannon a hug and then walked over to get his food. Before he reached the table, he turned around and came back over to Tiff. He whispered in her ear," I'll see you in a few minutes. Wait until it gets a little dark and then meet me at your truck." Then he just walked off, leaving her standing there blushing.

"Daddy! Daddy!" Ziaire said running to his dad.

EJ turned around and scooped his little man up. "What's up little man?"

"Where is my mommy at? I can't find her," Ziaire said hugging his dad.

"That boy has been looking for you and Yahnise ever since y'all pulled up," Ms. Pam said giving EJ a hug.

"I got him mom. Thanks. Is everybody enjoying themselves?" EJ said as he put his son down and grabbed some food.

"Yeah, look around you. Nobody is arguing, fighting, or killing each other. Thank God for that," Ms. Pam said.

"Well, let me take little man to see his mother. I'll see you later and don't be drinking up all the liquor," he said walking away.

Ms. Pam just sucked her teeth at him, because she already knew what she was going to do.

***

Later that day, everyone was starting to wind down from all the music, food, drinking, and partying that they were doing. Yahnise, Nyia, and Ms. Pam had taken all of the kids to see the fireworks at the Museum of Art. Chris, EJ, and Scrap had stayed back so they could talk about their next shipment. They were all sitting on the steps on the corner of Mellon Street.

"Pedro said that he wants to give us an additional ten keys tomorrow when we go see him," Chris said.

"Don't take them unless you are sure you can move them. That will be thirty keys of all pure dope that we will be flipping. Off of each key, we are now cutting them to twelve. That's three hundred sixty keys we will have to get rid of. We have the clientele to do it; we just have to up their product. I think we can handle it though," EJ said.

"Yeah, so that's all it is then. I'll give him a million in cash and I'll give him the other $200,000.00 later," Chris said as they watched a group of girls walk pass with some little ass shorts on with their asses hanging out.

"No, give him everything this time. I don't want to owe anybody anymore. Scrap will go with you to make sure you don't run into any trouble. The three other drivers will go straight to the WaWa, while you two meet Pedro at the spot. Tell him that I appreciate all of the business he is giving us," EJ said as he received a text message on his phone.

When he checked the message, it was Tiff informing him that she was at her truck waiting for him. He smirked and then finished his conversation with Scrap and Chris.

"Have you heard anything from any of Ed's people?" Scrap asked.

"So far, none of the spots have been touched since that situation was taken care of," Chris said.

"I knew he had something to do with that shit. That nigga cost us a substantial amount of money. If he wouldn't have been so greedy and twofaced, he would still be here eating like the rest of us. Well, I have to take care of something real quick.

136

You niggas chill and keep an eye out on things. I'll be back in about ten minutes or so," EJ said walking down the street.

Tiff was parked on the 3800 block of Mellon Street. When EJ got to her truck, she was sitting in there with her skirt and panties already off. EJ smiled and climbed in the backseat.

"I see you tried to start without me, huh? Let me help you with that," he said putting his face in between her legs and eating her pussy.

"That's what I'm talking about," Tiff said leaning back and enjoying the pleasure.

Tiff and EJ used to have sex once a month after Denver was killed. Lately, they had been all about business so they were not sexing each other as they used to. When she said she wanted some earlier, he realized that they hadn't had sex in months. He decided to do it for old times' sake. He never even tried to flirt with Shannon out of respect for Denver. He treated her more like a sister than anything else. She had keys to all of the spots, she knew his access codes to some of his accounts, and he told her shit that she knew he wouldn't even tell his own wife. That was their relationship, and Tiff benefited off of it just because they were close. Now she was getting some much-needed pleasure from her boss.

***

Scrap and Chris were still sitting on the steps smoking Loud when they saw two motorcycles passing the barricade that was still up. They really didn't pay any mind to them at first, until Scrap saw that the two people on the back were carrying what seemed to be sub-machine guns.

"CHRIS GET DOWN! IT'S A HIT!" Scrap yelled pulling Chris to the ground as the gunfire erupted.

They both pulled out to return fire, but the tow motorcycles were gone just as fast as they came. They looked at each other and wandered who that was, but most importantly, what was it all about?

EJ was fucking Tiff in the backseat when he heard the shots. He quickly pulled out and pulled his pants up looking out the window to see what was happening.

"What the fuck is going on out there?" Tiff asked throwing her skirt on without her panties. Then she grabbed her forty-five from the front seat.

EJ jumped out the car and ran down the street followed by Tiff. When they got to the corner and saw everybody that was cleaning up from the cookout, running around checking on others, they started doing the same.

Chris spotted EJ and called out to him. EJ went over to where Chris and Scrap were to make sure they were good.

"Who was that shooting?"

"We don't know! It was four people on two motorcycles. They weren't even trying to hit nobody. They shot in the air and took off around the corner," Chris said looking around for any signs of bullet holes.

"I bet you it was Ed's people trying to shake everybody up," Scrap said passing his gun to Tiff so she could go put it up. The others did the same as they saw the off duty cops on their radios looking around with their guns out trying to calm everyone down.

Police sirens were screaming from a distance as they saw flashing lights getting closer. "Let's bounce before they want to question everybody. Call the girls and let them know what happened. Tell them that we'll meet them at home," EJ said as he jumped in the car with Chris. His wife had the Aston Martin with her so he knew she was cool.

As they were riding down Lancaster Avenue, they saw that the cops had four people lying on the ground. The two motorcycles were parked at the club that they were outside of. "Pull over right here for a minute. Let's see how this plays out," EJ informed Chris.

They sat and watched the cops harass the four people for about twenty minutes. When they couldn't find anything to hold them on, they let them go. As the crowd laughed at the cops leaving, EJ noticed that one of the guys that was being searched, bent down and grabbed his sub-machine gun from under the tires of one of the cars. Then they went inside the club followed by the onlookers.

"That had to be them. Call Scrap, Shannon, and Tiff, and tell them where we are. Tell them to bring the big shit around here and hurry up," EJ said as Chris began dialing numbers.

***

Twenty minutes later, they were all sitting in Tiff's truck ready to hit the motorcycle club up.

"Why didn't they go home instead of sitting down the street from where they were just shooting?" Shannon asked.

"I don't get that part either, but they are gonna wish the cops would have taken them instead of what's about to pop off," Scrap said cocking the AR-15.

"There they go now about to leave," Chris said as they came out laughing about to get on their bikes.

"Let them have it, y'all," EJ said as they all jumped out the truck with Tiff still in the driver's seat.

They ran up on the four dudes before they could do anything and started cutting on them.

CLACK!

CLACK!

CLACK!

POP!

POP!

POP!

BOC!

BOC!

TAT!

TAT!

TAT!

Gunfire was all that was heard as the bodies fell over the bikes and on the pavement.

The other people that were inside the club still came running out with their straps just to be laid out too.

POP!

POP!

TAT!

TAT

TAT!

CLACK!

CLACK!

CLACK!

BOC!

BOC!

BOC!

"Let's bounce," Scrap yelled as they all jumped back in the truck. Tiff took off leaving everybody laid out in the front of the club.

"Take us over to Millick Street. We can chill there until Yahnise and Nyia go pick your car up, Chris. The rest of you can go home and chill for the night," EJ said taking off the latex gloves.

"If you come to shoot, you better kill the next time mutha-fuckas!" Scrap said all hyped up.

When they got to Millick Street, everybody got out and Tiff left to switch cars. EJ and Chris went inside the house to chill while Shannon started walking towards Scrap.

She grabbed his arm before he got into his whip. "Which way are you going?"

"I'm heading out to Delaware and stay at my house out there until we meet up with Pedro tomorrow," Scrap said.

"Can I go with you? I don't feel like staying at my place tonight. I need to be in the company of a man, if you know what I mean," she said looking at him seductively.

"I would love to do that, but wifey is home waiting for me. We can't even go someplace else because I already told her that I'm on my way. Can I get a rain check on it?"

"I'll think about it. I'll see you later, then," Shannon said walking away from him heading towards her ride.

"Damn! What a waste of a good piece of ass. I would have probably hurt that little pussy anyway," Scrap said out loud pulling off.

What Scrap didn't know was that turning some sweet pussy down tonight might have just saved his life.

Ed and one of his goons were waiting at Scrap's South Philly crib. Some girl that Ed was fucking was also fucking Scrap every time he stayed in Philly. She had told Ed over pillow talk about some dude that was getting money from Delaware. Ed was curious and decided to get her to set him up.

When she didn't want to do it, he gave her a stack (one thousand dollars) to tell him the address. She was money hungry so she instantly give him the address.

It was now 2:00 a.m., and Ed and his goon were still waiting. "Let's roll. That clown ass nigga ain't coming. We'll catch him some other time. Tomorrow my Plan B goes into motion," Ed said sniffing a line of Coke off the matchbook he was holding in his hand. His phone kept ringing, but he ignored it. If he had answered it, he would have known that his cousin had just been killed.

CHAPTER 22

No Way Out

At 9:00 the next morning, Chris, Scrap, and three of their workers were over in Delaware at the WaWa. Chris and Scrap left them there while they went to meet the connect at the West Inn. As they were turning out of the lot, an Escalade was turning in. Chris already knew who it was.

"Those niggas need to start switching their cars. If we wanted to rob them, they wouldn't be hard to find," Scrap said.

"I don't think you would want to do that, with all of the artillery those niggas carry. Plus, you may see that car, but you're not paying any attention to the other four that's sitting on each side of the street watching that one," Chris pointed out.

Scrap looked back and seen the formation that the cars were in, "Damn! That shit looks like something straight out of a gangster movie! That nigga Pedro don't play about his doe, huh?"

"That's why we are on our bullshit now. We can't let nothing penetrate what we have anymore. From now on, when niggas get close to us, they will pay the ultimate price; death," Chris said as they pulled into the West Inn.

They drove to the back where Pedro was waiting. He was sitting in his new Cadillac XTS 70 limo.

"This nigga is always in some bad ass limo shit. That's how I'mma start moving around," Chris said getting out the car.

He walked over and was patted down before getting into the car with Pedro who was sipping on his favorite drink.

"How is my friend EJ doing?"

"He's good and he sends his greetings. He also said that he doesn't mind snatching the thirty up," Chris said.

"So I guess he is now one of the top suppliers on the East Coast thanks to me, huh?" Pedro said feeling good knowing that his product had the whole US on lock.

Nobody knew it, but Pedro wasn't even the real boss. He was only the son and middleman to the biggest Cartel in the history of the United States. Everyone thought they were dealing with the boss because he traveled everywhere to supply the bigtime dealer's. It would never be that easy to get to a real boss.

Even if you tried to get at Pedro, you better come correct. He had over fifty men with him everywhere he went. Right now, there were several different sharp shooters scattered around watching with military style high power riffles. If anything went wrong, the culprit would be dead before he could say, "Give it up." Pedro was a good man and he believed in giving everyone a chance, except the ones who had burnt their bridges with him.

"We have the whole one point two million for you. That way, we don't owe you anything," Chris said as he watched the two guards taking the two duffle bags out of the trunk.

"Now, that's how I like doing business. Tell EJ next time we meet, there will be an additional ten, along with his order for free. I wish I could stay longer, but I have a plane to catch. You drive safely back to Philadelphia and always be alert," Pedro said shaking Chris' hand.

Chris exited the limo and jumped back in his car. They pulled out of the lot heading back towards WaWa. "Everything went good I see," Scrap said.

"Hell yeah and he offered us another ten free keys on our next re-up."

"Did you just say free?" Scrap asked cheering up.

"Damn right, that's what I said. Wait until I tell EJ about this shit," Chris said sounding excited.

"Do you really have to say anything to EJ? Why can't we just split that shit between us? That would be a come up and a half for us," Scrap said letting greed cloud his better judgment.

Chris looked at him and started thinking about all the extra money that he would have if he cut and flipped the extra ten keys himself. Then he thought about how good his brother-in-law had treated him. Did he really want to bite the hand that's been feeding him?"

Scrap saw him in deep thought and said, "That will be two point four million apiece for each of us off of it."

"I'll think about it, but we will really have to be discrete about it. I cannot have him after me for some bullshit," Chris said.

"He will never find out because we can get rid of them all in DC and Atlanta. I already have buyers to take them because they already heard about Numbers and wanted to cop from EJ. We can just say that we are bringing it to them for him. They won't know the difference because EJ never deals with people face to face anymore anyway," Scrap said.

He didn't even feel one ounce of guilt from betraying the one person who had put him on. It was all a part of the game.

"Let me think about it for a while. Besides, we have until next month when we re-up anyway. I'll let you know," Chris said as they headed home with the three-stash cars behind them.

***

"Did you get all that?" Agent Kaplin asked the other agent who was snapping shot after shot the whole time.

"Yes Sir. I got it all. I even got the spy cars that were watching. Do you see how organized they are?" the young agent asked.

"I see it, but they're not that organized because in about another month they will all be sitting behind bars, even the one that's sitting in that limo. I know it has to be Pedro. His father will never come to the states and show his face, that's why we can't catch him yet," Agent Kaplin said.

"Do you want me to follow them to see where they are going?"

"No, that's okay. We already know where they are going. Let's get back to headquarters so we can file the evidence we have," Agent Kaplin said.

Agent Kaplin knew he had a solid cause against EJ and his crew. He just wanted a little more. He knew exactly whom he would get it from too.

***

"Attention all areas! Attention all areas! US Marshalls with one in the Sally Port!"

They had finally flown Mr. Donnie Stevens back to Delaware, so that he could face the music for killing the State Trooper that had tried to pull him over.

As soon as he walked in the booking and receiving and Gander Hill, everybody was looking at the infamous cop killer. The Marshall's unshackled him and they put him in a holding cell until the C/O's were ready to process him.

Loud Pack looked around at the walls in the cell. He knew that this would be his home for the rest of his life. He already wished he wouldn't have come out of the motel so soon. He got greedy wanting to buy new clothes and splurge in the new city a little. That was a costly mistake that he wished he could take back, but he couldn't.

"Stevens," the desk Sergeant said snapping Loud Pack out of his daydream.

He walked over to the desk and filled out some paperwork that they had for him. He was then strip-searched and given white D.O.C.'s to wear. After that, they gave him an orange wristband. It has his picture, name, date of birth, and inmate number on it. Once Loud Pack was finished being processed, the C/O gave him a bedroll and put him back in the holding cell.

"Can I please have my phone call now?" Loud Pack asked the C/O.

"After your visitor leaves. Someone is coming to see you," she said and then walked off.

Forty-five minutes later, the female C/O came and escorted Loud Pack to a room, to see his visitor. When Loud Pack walked in, Agent Kaplin was sitting there smiling at him.

"What the fuck do you want, Pig?" Loud Pack asked in an angry tone.

"Sit your dumb ass down and find out," Agent Kaplin told him.

"Donnie Stevens," he begin. "It seems to me that you got yourself in a real jam. I can help you out if you help me. Just think of me as your *Captain Save a Ho*."

"I don't know what you are insinuating, but the conversation is now over, mutha-fucka! I wish I would rat someone out. You can go to hell with your deal and take all those other niggas that turned into rats with you," Loud Pack said looking at Agent Kaplin.

"You know what? I hope your dumb ass rots in jail, you piece of shit! As a matter of fact, I don't even know why I came here. You're a stupid nig---" Before he could get the word out, Loud Pack was on his ass.

Loud Pack hit the agent with a roundhouse and then an upper cut that lifted him up off of his feet. The agent fell on the floor and Loud Pack started stomping him out with his white Bob Barker's.

A C/O was walking past, taking inmates back to their housing units when he seen the Agent getting trashed. "Oh shit!" he said grabbing his radio.

"CODE ONE B&R! CODE ONE B&R!" he yelled in his radio while rushing in to help the Agent.

"Attention all areas! Attention all areas! Code one in booking in receiving," the C/O in Primary Control said over the PA system.

Not even thirty seconds later, ten officers came storming in the room punching on Loud Pack trying to help the Agent. Loud Pack was trying to fight all of them, but he was no match. They beat the shit out of him, worse than he did the agent.

After they subdued Loud Pack, the C/O cuffed him and then took him over to medical before taking him to solitary confinement. Agent Kaplin suffered a broken nose, and a few scratches, but other than that, he was okay.

***

Yahnise had just left from the club and was on her way to pick up Ziaire from her cousin's house. She had some early morning deliveries that she had to be there for so she had asked Alicia to pick him up from the daycare.

As she was driving down Huntington Park, a black van was following right behind her. In that van was the man and girl that had been saving Ed every time he got into a dangerous situation. They had brought along a third person just in case they needed him.

Yahnise pulled up in front of Alicia's house and left the car running as she stepped out. When she knocked on the door, her cousin came and opened it up, "Hey girl. Where is my bad boy at?"

"Come on in, I was just making him a sandwich, but he can take it with him," Alicia said heading back in the kitchen.

"Okay, hurry up because I have my car still running. I see they finally delivered your new furniture," Yahnise said looking at the new living room set.

"Yeah, they dropped it off yesterday. If you stop being a stranger and come around more, you would have already known that."

Yahnise sucked her teeth at her cousin while she put Ziaire's sneakers back on. "I told you, that I don't like coming down here. I wish you would just move somewhere else. It's a lot of weird people out this way," she said.

"That's everywhere, so get over it," Alicia said giving both of her cousin's a hug as they headed for the door.

"Call me Saturday morning so we can go shopping and get you something to wear for girl's night out next week."

"I sure the hell will. I'll see y'all then. Love you," she said shutting the door as they headed for their car.

Yahnise opened the back door as a man and a lady were walking past her. She wasn't paying them any attention as they passed right by her. She was about to buckle Ziaire in the backseat when someone grabbed her from behind. She tried to scream, but he covered her mouth with a cloth filled with Chloroform.

By the time the van pulled up, she was unconscious. They put her in the can and the girl grabbed the little boy who immediately started crying. Alicia was opening her curtains when she saw them throwing Ziaire in the van.

She ran out the door as the van was pulling off. She tried to get the plate number, but the van turned the corner. She jumped in Yahnise's car and grabbed her cell phone trying to call EJ. They had snatched her keys out of the ignition so she couldn't even chase after them. She didn't get an answer so she texted him, 911 and waited. Somebody was about to pay with their life for taking her cousins. Alicia damn sure wasn't calling the cops because she didn't fuck with the pigs. She just hoped that EJ would hurry up and call back so she could give him the information.

CHAPTER 23

A Love Lost

It had been twenty-four hours since the abduction of EJ's wife and son and he hadn't heard anything from anybody yet. All types of thoughts were going through his mind. Are they dead? Are they hurt? He tried to block all of the thoughts out of his mind, but the thoughts and the pain were just unbearable. Ever since EJ had got off the phone with Alicia, he had been riding around trying to make some kind of since of this whole situation.

He was trying to figure out who would want to kidnap his family. He didn't want to get the cops involved, so it was going to be all about street justice. If it's money that they want, then it's money that they will get. The problem with that was that no one had called with any demands.

EJ's crew had been out searching all night long. He was thinking about shutting the whole operation down until his wife and son were found, but in the end, he decided against it. Everybody was a suspect in his eyes, so he had to keep an eye on anybody or anything that looked suspicious. There was one person that came to his mind and that was Ed.

EJ was thinking to himself, "Would he go that far, even though he said their families were off limits?" All kinds of scenarios were running through his head. He felt his life would come to an end to save his family. He pulled over and picked up the Mack 11 on the passenger seat.

He rolled the windows down and called out to the group of dealer's that were standing near a house. "Have any of you seen Ed?"

"Who the fuck are you? Are you the cops or something? Man get the fuck out of here," one of them said.

"I'm a friend of his and it's really important that I catch up with him, so can you tell me where I can find him?" EJ said trying to be polite one more time.

The boy turned around, "You still here? If you don't get up out of here, I'm going to put all types of holes in that pretty ass car of yours," he said lifting up his shirt showing EJ the chrome gun in his waistband.

EJ had enough of the boy's smart mouth. Without saying a word, EJ jumped out of his car and started spraying everybody out there. They all hit the ground, and he ran up on them hitting them some more killing all but one of them.

He walked over to him and said, "Tell Ed I'm looking for him." With that, he ran back to his car and pulled off.

***

The police were on high alert because of all of the murders, especially the murders of the cops. That alone had everyone on the edge, so if someone even looked like they were carrying a weapon and a passing by officer seen you, they were on your ass. Some of them even used the code of the streets, "Shoot first and ask questions last," as a way of protecting themselves.

Officer Brandon Marshall was just leaving the precinct and was on his way to his 2014 Dodge Ram. To the average eye, he was just a normal hard working peaceful officer going home to his family. Deep down inside though, he was as corrupt as they came.

As he was about to enter his truck, a Dodge Magnum pulled up beside him. The driver rolled the window down as the officer looked inside. "Is everything taken care of?" the driver asked.

"Yeah the package is at the old N.O.B. (Night on Broadway) club. We were just waiting to see what the next move would be."

"Okay, I'll take it from here. You stay loyal and you will make a lot of money fucking with me. That other snake fucked up, and got caught slipping so he got what he deserved. Grab that bag out of my backseat," the driver said unlocking the doors to his car.

Officer Marshall went to open the back door. As soon as he pulled it open, he never saw it coming.

PHHH!

PHHH!

PHHH!

PHHH!

All of the shots hit him in the face as he fell back onto his truck. The tint was so dark that he didn't even see the figure sitting in the backseat of the car waiting for him. The driver sped off with about ten seconds to spare before a couple of other cops that were getting off, walked out, and noticed their dead comrade.

Officer Marshall was the one who helped assist in the abduction of EJ's family. They thought that he would be a liability so they decided to terminate his contract. In this deadly game they were playing, loose ends could and would be your downfall, which means loose ends could get you killed. That was a chance they weren't willing to take.

***

EJ finally made it home after being out searching for his wife and son. He had put a $100,000.00 reward out for anyone who could give them information on his family's whereabouts or the location of Ed. He was exhausted, but he refused to rest until he found Yahnise and Ziaire.

As he walked to the kitchen to get something to drink, his cellphone started ringing. He looked at the caller ID, but it was unavailable. "Hello," EJ said answering it anyway.

All he heard was silence on the other end. "HELLO! WHO THE FUCK IS THIS? DON'T BITCH UP NOW! YOU CALLED ME, SO SPEAK YOUR MIND!" he screamed into the phone getting tired of the suspense.

The caller hung up leaving EJ looking at his phone, hoping they would call back. A couple of minutes passed and then his phone rang again.

"Hello. I'm here," EJ said in a much calmer voice.

"That's more like it. You are not in charge, I am. I want you to listen carefully because I will not be repeating myself. I am willing to trade your family's life for yours. This offer is not negotiable, so if we have a deal, I will call you tomorrow night with the location of the meet. Don't worry, I will take care of your precious wife," the caller said and then hung up again before EJ could say anything.

"FUCK! I'MMA KILL EVERY LAST ONE OF YOU INVOLVED!" EJ screamed into a silent phone as he flipped the kitchen table over.

He knew exactly who had his wife and son now. He quickly dialed Scrap's number. When Scrap answered the phone he said, "Ed has my family. I will meet you at the stash house tomorrow at 3 p.m. Tell everybody to be ready because the city is about to be covered in blood."

"We will be ready for whatever. Just get some rest, man. You will need it. I'll handle everything on this end. I have ten niggas coming in from Rose Gate. They all are stone cold killers and they don't mind murking anybody that gets in the way," Scrap said.

"Good, because from this moment on, it's on sight for anybody playing the other side. I don't care who it is, everything and everybody is fair game," EJ said hanging up the phone and throwing it on the counter.

EJ knew his family wasn't going to walk out of there alive. Ed was the one who said families were off limits and now his word didn't mean shit. EJ knew one thing though, if he was going to die, so was Ed.

***

Over on Broad and Oleny, in the old N.O.B. building. Yahnise was tied to a stripper pole, laying on a mattress. She only had on panties and a bra. Her eyes were blindfolded and her mouth was gagged. Yahnise could feel someone watching her, but they wouldn't say anything.

After playing the waiting game for about ten minutes, Ed approached her and removed her blindfold.

When she saw him, she started squirming trying to break free. Tears were in her eyes as she kept mumbling something. "Mwwwwww."

"What was that? I can't hear you," Ed said mocking her. "Let me remove this from over your mouth so I can understand you," he said taking the gag from her mouth.

"Where's my son, you fucking psycho? Please just let us go! We didn't do anything to you!"

"Yeah, you didn't, but your husband murdered my mom. He's gonna pay for that shit too. You and your son will be my bargaining chip to get him here. He thinks that I'm going to let you go for his life, but I'm going to do something special before I do," Ed said looking at Yahnise's body as if she was a piece of meat.

"If you think you're going to rape me, I'd rather die first," Yahnise spat.

Ed just laughed at her irrational way of thinking. "I thought you would be more acceptable to my rules, but it seems like you will need some persuasion in this matter. See you don't know how many countless times I wanted your curvaceous body for myself, but you chose EJ."

"That's because I love him and you will never be able to amount up to the man that he is. You may try to take my body, but you will never have my heart."

"We'll see about that after you try some of the product I stole from your husband's stash houses," Ed said as he took out a needle and a red pack of the Blood Game dope that he had stolen from EJ.

He begin to cook it on a spoon with a lighter. Next, he filled up the needle and walked over to Yahnise. Ed took off his belt and wrapped it around her arm. When he went to insert the needle in her arm, she kept moving and screaming, "DON'T PUT THAT SHIT IN ME! SOMEBODY HELP ME, PLEASE!"

Since he couldn't get a clear vein to insert it in her arm, Ed stuck the needle through her panties and into her pussy. As soon as he injected the heroin into her body, she relaxed as the sensation took over her sane mind. It felt so good to her, that she had an orgasm.

"That's right baby. Calm down and let me take care of you. I know exactly what you need," Ed said as he pulled out two Molly's from his pocket and ripped her panties off.

Ed took the Molly's and stuffed them in her ass making her squirm a little. It didn't take long for the affect to kick in. The heroin and the Molly's made Yahnise horny as hell. She didn't know didn't know who was inside of her. All she knew was that she wanted more and more sex.

Ed was fucking her in the missionary position hard and fast. After he busted all over her body, he got up and walked to the door. "Y'all niggas get in here and have a little bit of this good pussy."

The two goons that were watching at first, went over to the stage where Yahnise was all tied up, laying on the mattress and took turns having their way with her. She was so fucked up that she didn't know she was getting raped.

Three hours later, Yahnise heard someone asking her if she was hungry. She was drowsy and sore from the drugs and gang rape. She couldn't remember anything that had happened. All she remembered was being stuck with a needle.

"Are you hungry Yahnise? You have to eat something," the voice said again.

That voice sounded so familiar to her, but she couldn't see a face because it was pitch black from the blindfold over her face. All she knew was that it was a female's voice. Her body felt wet and sticky and she could fell that she didn't have any panties on which proved to her that she had been raped.

"Well, I'll come back in a few minutes. I'll try to find something to cover you up, okay," the female said as he was about to walk away.

"Wait! Please don't leave me here like this," Yahnise said.

The female came back over and sat down next to the bed. She took a wet rag and wiped her face.

"Can I have something to drink, please? My mouth is real dry," she said to the woman.

Yahnise was really just trying to stall a little bit so that she could hear the female's voice some more. She couldn't get over how familiar her voice sounded.

The woman put the straw to Yahnise's mouth and she sipped the water from the container. "I will come back in a couple of minutes with something to cover you up in. Don't worry, I won't be gone long."

"Where is Ed at?" Yahnise asked.

"He had to take care of something, but he'll be back soon. You just sit tight and once we get your husband, we will let you go."

Just as if someone had slapped the shit out of Yahnise, that voice finally came to her. She just couldn't believe that out of all the people on her man's team, it was she.

"Shannon, is that you? Why would you betray EJ like that? You were like our family."

"Well, I guess you don't need these on anymore," Shannon said as she took the blindfold off of Yahnise. "How could I not be on my baby father's side? After this, he made a promise to me that we would be a family. I was tired of riding around every day watching your man try to kill mines. If Ed dies, my son won't have a father anymore. How do you think it felt, that I had to pretend that the next nigga was my child's father? Do you know how confusing that can get for my son? Well not anymore, because when EJ dies, we will take over everything including the heroin industry," Shannon said looking at Yahnise.

"What about me and Ziaire? If you kill EJ, we won't have a husband and a father. Do you really think ---," she said before being cut off.

"Fuck your family! I can care less what happens to your spoiled rotten ass. It's all about my family and me now. Besides, you're not going to make it out of here alive anyway. Once Ed kills EJ and that crying ass son of yours, you will be the next one to go. We won't leave any witnesses when we're done," Shannon said smiling.

"Please Shannon, let me see my son. I just want to make sure that he is all right. I'm asking you mother to mother," Yahnise begged.

"Come on with that soft ass shit! All that shit you're talking won't make me change my mind! Fuck your son! I should kill that little bastard now!" she said looking into Yahnise's glassy eyes.

"Why would you help the person that killed your cousins?"

Shannon slapped the shit out of Yahnise! "They were in the wrong place at the wrong time. They knew what came with selling drugs. You are either going to die, or you are going to prison!"

Yahnise couldn't believe how Shannon was acting. Why had nobody figured out that she was a snake? "What made you turn your back on EJ? He treated you like a partner in this business and family. You still never said the real reason you turned on him," Yahnise said trying to keep her talking while she figured out how to get out of there.

"You want to know the real reason, well I'll tell you. He was fucking my sister before she was murdered, but he would never look at me like that. I even tried to dress really provocative and he still wouldn't even try. I see you and y'all happy family and I wanted it. That's why," she said angrily.

"So that's why your man drugged and raped me?" Yahnise asked.

"Oh so you want to lie, huh? I'll teach you to try and lie on my man! He wouldn't dare put his dick in you! Take it back now or you will wish that you never said it!"

"Bitch, how dumb are you? Look at me and tell me that I haven't been raped! I have that niggas semen all over my body. You can play like you're that damn stupid all you want, but he's gonna get his just like you will get yours," Yahnise said. She could see that she had gotten under Shannon's skin so she pushed further. "How naïve can you be dumbass? My husband will never love anyone but me while your little boyfriend is a no good cheating rapist! Your little son will be a rapist and a bastard when he gets older if he follows in his father's footsteps.

That was the breaking point for Shannon. "You want to see your son? I'll let you see him for this one last time. It's the least I can do," she said as she walked away from the stage.

Yahnise started crying tears of joy as she waited to see her little man. She just hoped that her big man would hurry up and save them. She started itching because her body was craving some more dope. That feeling made her feel like she was in another place. "Please God, send my knight to save me," she said looking to the sky.

"Mommy! Mommy! Mommy!" she heard Ziaire screaming. She looked up and saw her son running towards her. She was smiling and crying at the same time as she watched him climbing the steps to the stage.

POP!

POP!

POP!

POP!

Was all that was heard as everything happened in slow motion. One minute Ziaire was running to her calling her name and the next he was lying in a pool of blood and Shannon was holding the smoking gun.

"NOOOOOOOO!" Yahnise screamed seeing her son dead on the stage a few feet away from her.

"Now whose son is the bastard, bitch?!" Shannon said with an evil look on her face.

Ed and the two goons heard the shots and came running with their guns in their hands. As soon as he seen the little boy lying dead in a puddle of blood, he looked at Shannon. "What did you do that for?"

"She made me do it, talking about you raped her. I did it to teach her a lesson," she said still standing there with the gun in her hand and a blank look on her face.

Ed looked at Yahnise and then back at Shannon. "Oh well, that's one less body for tomorrow. You two, clean this mess up, and fast."

"You go out there and chill out for a while," he said taking the gun from Shannon.

"NOOOOOO! WHY DID YOU KILL MY BABY? NOT MY BABY! OH GOD, NOOOO!" Yahnise kept screaming.

Ed went up on the stage and grabbed her mouth. She kept screaming and crying. He took out the needle and heroin from his pocket. He cooked up the dope and put it in the needle. Then he stuck it in the same place as before to shut her up.

It took effect immediately and it calmed her down. Ed took his outer shirt off leaving on his wife beater and covered her up. He looked at the two goons wrapping up the little kids body. "If she wakes up acting hysterical, give her another shot. have to go take care of something."

Ed thought to himself, *"Damn, this shit has just gotten real. There's no turning back from this point on."*

CHAPTER 24

Tragedy Turned Triumph

The next morning EJ woke up from the sound of the doorbell ringing. He had fallen asleep on the couch last night. He got up to answer the door, when his heart started beating fast. He didn't known why, but he felt like something wasn't right.

When he answered the door, he had the forty caliber by his side. When he opened up the door, it was Sonja standing there. "Can I come in, please?" she asked.

EJ just walked away from the door as she followed him into the living room. She looked around and noticed that the table and chairs were flipped over.

EJ sat on the couch. "What do you want?"

"I heard what happened to Yahnise and I'm here to help you if you let me. She is my friend too," she said as tears came down her face.

"And just how in the hell do you expect to help me? Have you talked to somebody in the streets that I haven't talked to that might know the whereabouts of my wife and son? If not, then you are just in my mutha-fucking way!"

Sonja could see that he had been crying all night. "I can't imagine how you are feeling right now and I won't try to, but I want you to hear me out because I have to tell you something important," she said.

"Talk! I'm listening," he said staring out into space.

As soon as she was about to begin, his phone rang. He looked down at it and saw that it was Scrap. "What's up? Tell me something good, bro."

"We have a location on one of Ed's cribs that they might have them at. It's an apartment in Karmen Suites on Island Avenue. Do you want us to go in, or wait it out and see what happens?" Scrap said.

"Sit tight until I get there. Anything unusual happens call me ASAP! I'm jumping on the road now. I should be there in about forty-five minutes or less," EJ said as he hung up the phone. He looked at Sonja as he checked his forty caliber and grabbed four extra clips off of the table. "I'm sorry, but that conversation will have to wait until some other time. I have a serious matter that needs to be addressed right now," he said heading for the door.

"Let me go with you, EJ! I can help!" she said grabbing her purse.

"Do you know how to shoot a gun? Have you ever even held a gun in your hand or better yet, killed someone before? This shit that I'm about to do is not a fucking game. I can't have someone getting in my way that may get killed in the process," he said looking at her.

Sonja pulled out a P90 Glock. "I can hold my own. Let's go," she said not giving EJ a chance to comment. The two jumped in the all black tinted out GMS Terrain. No music or words were spoken the whole ride to Philly. EJ was thinking about revenge and getting his wife and son back while Sonja was trying to figure out a way to tell him the important information that she was holding back on.

***

Yahnise woke up feeling groggy from all of the heroin that they had shot up in her. She looked around for a couple of minutes trying to figure out did she just have a horrible dream or did she really just see her son get shot right before her eyes. Thoughts of his last words, "Mommy! Mommy! Mommy!" ran back through her mind. She remembered it like it all had just happened again.

"Mommy! Mommy! Mommy!" Ziaire screamed running up the steps of the stage and then all of a sudden, POP! POP! POP! POP! Ziaire fell right on his face from the four bullets entering his body.

"NOOOOOOO!" Yahnise screamed as she replayed the scenario of her son dying right before her eyes and just only a couple of feet away from hugging her.

Those memories would haunt her for the rest of her life. The only thing on her mind right now was getting her hands on Shannon. She had taken her only child away from her without even flinching. If she could ever get out of this, she made a vow to herself that she would kill her with her bare hands.

The sound of footsteps broke Yahnise from her thoughts. She looked up and saw one of Ed's men walking her way. As he got close to the stage, Yahnise could see in his eyes what he had in mind.

He walked up on the stage and removed the shirt that covered the lower part of her body exposing her pussy. He started licking his lips and rubbing himself as he stared at her.

"Please don't rape me again! My husband will pay you triple the amount of whatever Ed is paying you if you let me go," Yahnise said hoping his greed would make him reconsider.

You could tell that the thought entered his mind by the way he momentarily froze in place. She decided to keep trying.

"I'll even tell him that you didn't have anything to do with our son getting killed and that you were the one who saved my life. You will walk away a rich man without any repercussions."

"Mmmmm, that offer sounds good, but how about you throw an extra incentive in the deal?" he said licking his lips.

She knew what he wanted by the way he was looking at her, holding his dick. She thought about it for a minute, and if that were what it would take to get out of here, then so be it.

"How do I know that you won't try to renege on your word?" she asked.

"You don't. You will just have to trust me. I want five million dollars wired to my account overseas and I want to fuck that beautiful body of yours one more time, and I want you to guarantee me that your husband won't kill me," he said.

She started smiling because she knew this nigga was a pussy. Any other nigga would have just taken what they wanted, but he was trying to cop a deal. Yahnise knew she had him where she wanted him, so she decided to play on his weakness. "You have a deal," she said with a smile.

"I'll be back in one hour and if you are serious, you'll be a free woman and I'll be a rich man," he said.

"Why can't you just let me go now? I promise, I will not burn you," she said in a pleading manner.

"I have to wait for Shannon to leave first," he said covering her back up with the shirt.

The thought of Shannon killing her son came back like a sharp pain. "Please tell me what y'all did with my son's body."

He looked at her for a moment before responding, "We wrapped him in a sheet and put him out with the rest of the garbage."

At that moment, Yahnise said to herself that she would kill him as soon as he let her go. Her brain was now in survival mode and she thought about everything that EJ and her father had taught her. She was going to get out of this alive.

***

When EJ and Sonja pulled up to Karmen Suite's Apartment complex, Scrap, Chris, Tiffany, and ten killers dressed in all black with all types of automatic weapons were sitting in two vans waiting for them. Chris and Scrap stepped out of the van and walked over to EJ as he got out of the truck.

"So where is this nigga at?" EJ asked with a murderous look in his eyes.

"They are in apartment 1-A. We saw two people go in, but no one came out. I suspect that it's at least four niggas in there," Chris said with Scrap agreeing.

"Okay, since they are on the first floor, it shouldn't be hard to get all of them. If my wife and son are in there, we have to do this without bringing any harm to them. They will try to put my family in the line of fire, and I just can't have that. Did anybody see Ed's bitch ass come in or out?"

"No, if he's in there, then he has been in there since I got here. I think we should use a different approach. We can get Tiff to knock on the door and ask for Ed. If he's not there, then we'll get her to act like she needs something and then see how it plays out," Scrap said.

"Okay, send half of the goons around the back and then the others will surround the front, but stay out of sight because it's too bright out here. If any of the neighbors see them, I'm sure they will call the pigs so let's get in and out," Chris said.

He and Scrap were more built for this killer shit than EJ was. They had been doing it ever since they were young. EJ on the other hand, had gotten his first kill after his friend Maria was killed in a shootout outside of Trilogy, trying to save him on his birthday.

Scrap called Tiffany out of the car. She had on some real tight short denim shorts and a wife beater. She walked over and gave EJ a hug. "Sorry about your wife, but we're going to get her back."

"Thank you! You just be careful, okay. As soon as they open the door, we'll be on their ass so don't panic," EJ told her.

"Don't worry, I got this," Tiff said walking towards the door.

When Tiffany rang the doorbell for apartment 1-A, she could see somebody peeping through the window. A couple of seconds later, a man opened the door. "What's good, Ma? What you need?" he asked.

"I'm looking for Ed. He told me that I could come through whenever I wanted to see him," Tiff said seductively.

"Well, he's not here, but me and my homie's are. Would you like to chill with us?" he said letting his dick talk for him.

"Well, as long as I'm here, I might as well have a little fun," she said as the dude opened the door wider inviting her in.

As soon as Tiff stepped inside, she had her gun out in a flash. Scrap, Chris, and EJ rushed through the door with four of the goons in tow. They grabbed two of the niggas before they could even react.

"Don't move or you are dead!" Scrap said with a gun to one of the men's head.

Tiff had the one that had opened the door for her on his knees, while EJ was pointing his gun at another nigga. They moved through the house with so much precision that the men didn't know what had hit them.

The fourth nigga was in the bathroom and he tried to climb through the window, when he was met by two AK 47's pointed at his head. They pulled him the rest of the way out the window and walked him to the door. Once of the goons opened up the door letting him in.

"Now that we are all here, I'm going to ask you a question. If I don't get the answer that I'm looking for, a body will fall," EJ said.

"Nigga, you can ask what you want, but I'm not saying shit," the one that Tiff had her gun on said.

EJ gave Tiff a nod and she put a hole through his head.

BOOM!

Once he fell, she put two more shots in his heart.

BOOM!

BOOM!

"Now he has no brains or heart," she said with a smirk on her face.

"Where is my wife and son being held at? Before you answer that question, I'm going to warn you, falsified statements will get you death penalty. Now you can answer the question," EJ said waiting.

The scared nigga that EJ had his gun on had already pissed his pants. "I, I, I, don, don't know what you're talk ---," that was as far as he got.

BOC!

BOC!

BOC!

EJ put three in his head. "Wrong fucking answer," he said as the man's body hit the floor.

"We really don't know anything," the other man said pleading for his life.

EJ knew they had to be telling the truth because if they knew something, they would have been spitting it out by now or they were some loyal soldiers. Either way, EJ knew they would be calling Ed as soon as they left and that would really put his family in great danger. So with just a head nod, they finished the other two off.

They left out the door and took off before the cops came. They knew that the other tenants had heard gunshots, so it wouldn't be long before this place would be swarming with cops.

Sonja heard the shots as she sat there with her gun in her hand. She was about to get out of the car when she saw EJ and his crew rush out the door and jump in their vehicles. She relaxed back in the seat, hiding her phone between her legs.

***

Forty-five minutes had went past and Yahnise still hadn't heard from Ed's flunky. Truth be told, she was kind of hoping that her husband would find and save her before he came back. Her arms and legs were in pain from being tied up so long and her mouth was dry form not enough nourishment and she knew that she needed a bath because she could smell herself.

Yahnise started crying, but no tears would come out because her heart was cold. She wanted her son back, and as much as he knew he was gone, she believed he was still alive. What hurt her even more was the fact that once EJ found out that his little man was gone; he really was going to lose it. All hell was about to break loose and she hoped that she would be there when he put a bullet through Ed's head.

The door opened and in came Ed's goon. He was carrying a bottle in his hand and he looked like he was drunk. As he got closer, she noticed that he was staggering, and could smell the liquor coming out of his pores. He walked up and sat on the mattress next to her.

"So are you really going to let me go?"

He looked at her and then put his hand on one of her thighs. "If I get what I want, then and only then will you get out of here," he said moving the shirt exposing her bottom half.

Yahnise knew that this was it and she had to work fast so she could escape before anyone else came. It was time to seduce this gullible ass nigga and get up out of here.

"Come on baby, I need you to untie me so I can hold you while you fuck this tight pussy you've been yearning for," she said licking her dry lips.

The man put his bottle of liquor down and stood up. "I will only untie your hands; okay?"

"I need to be all the way free so I can let you hit this doggy style and I can suck on that big dick of yours."

That really got his attention as he started to untie the rope. When he released her from the pole, she started rubbing her waist. "So, let's see what you got, little lady," he said lying on the bed.

Yahnise seductively stood up and removed her bra. She moved back on the bed and stood over top of him. "Close your eyes baby because I'm about to give you something you will never forget."

"Oh shit! That's right girl! I knew you wanted some more of this good dick!" he said closing his eyes.

Yahnise grabbed the bottle as she sat down on his dick without letting it penetrate her. In one swift motion, she swung the bottle at his head dazing him. She hit him again and again until the bottle broke over his head.

"AHHHH! AHHHHHHHHH! AHHHH!"

Pain and agony was all that could be heard from the man before he was knocked unconscious.

Then she took the neck of the broken bottle and stabbed him repeatedly in his chest where his heart was. Blood was squirting all over her, but she wouldn't stop until her arms got tired. She stood up and started searching his pants for a phone. She couldn't find one, so she grabbed the Jersey and put it on and then she started walking towards the door.

When she peeked out, she didn't see anybody. She ran through the building and down the steps trying to get out. When she tried to open the door, it was locked.

"FUCK! I got to get out of here!" she said to no one in particular.

She ran back upstairs remembering that she had felt some keys in the dead man's pocket. As she got the keys and headed back to the door, Shannon was coming up the steps. Yahnise hid behind the counter so she didn't see her.

As soon as she walked pass, Yahnise jumped out and grabbed her by her hair.

"BITCH, I TOLD YOU I WAS GONNA KILL YOU WITH MY BARE HANDS!" Yahnise screamed as she punched Shannon in the stomach and head repeatedly.

Shannon stumbled and fell backwards. When she got back to her feet, she reached for her gun under her shirt. As she took it out, Yahnise charged into her, knocking it out of her hand. "No bitch! It's just me an you now!" she said.

"So let's do it then," Shannon said standing up.

She tried to swing and Yahnise ducked the punch and then came up with an uppercut to the chin and then a jab to her face. Then she pulled her by her head and smashed her face into the mirror that was hanging on the wall.

Shannon fell to the ground and Yahnise kicked her repeatedly in the stomach. As Yahnise was about to walk away, Shannon grabbed her leg making her fall on her face. "My turn, bitch! I'm going to beat you senseless and then put a bullet through your skull like I did your crying ass son," Shannon said heading towards the gun.

Yahnise found enough strength to get up and tackle Shannon to the ground trying to stop her from reaching the gun.

They struggled and fought for the gun like two caged animals. They both had a hand on the gun when it suddenly went off.

"BOC!

Both women fell to the ground. No one moved at first until Yahnise pulled Shannon off of her. She stood up with the gun in hand and looked at Shannon holding her stomach.

"Bitch, I told you that you were gonna get yours!"

BOC!

BOC!

BOC!

BOC!

BOC!

BOC!

"THAT'S FOR MY SON, BITCH! I HATE YOU! I HATE YOU! I HATE YOU!" Yahnise screamed as she kicked the dead corpse.

Yahnise looked in Shannon's purse and found her car keys. She ran out the door and jumped in Shannon's car. She started the car and pulled it around the back to the alley. She was looking for her son.

She pulled up next to a dumpster and jumped out crying. She ran over looking inside for Ziaire. The first dumpster was empty so she looked over in the second one. When she got to the second one, her heart stopped.

She found Ziaire wrapped in a sheet with blood all over it. She quickly lifter her son out of the dumpster and placed him gently in the backseat. She jumped in the car and pulled off. She was so in shock that she didn't even know where she was going. One thing for sure, she needed to find her husband. She forgot to grab Shannon's cell phone in all of the commotion. She just drove crying her heart out.

CHAPTER 25

Reunited

"Agent Kaplin, wait up," one of the agents said running to catch up to him before he got in his car.

"What's up, Jim?"

"I just got off the phone with one of our field agents. Something big is going down in Southwest and it's going down now," he said out of breath.

"Is that one of the areas where Edward or Eric is?"

"Yes, that is what I'm talking about. The local police were dispatched there about thirty minutes ago, and it's the same location our field agent called from. They reported shots from heavy artillery being fired," he said.

"I want you to get a team together and get over there now. Hit my phone up, and let me know whatever you find out. I'm about to go check on another lead that I just received," Agent Kaplin said.

"What you find out?" he questioned.

"I receive another call from the police department over on Broad and Champlost. They told me they found two bodies. One was beat and shot multiple times, and the other one was stabbed in the chest repeatedly. This happened inside of the old strip club on Broad and Oleny called Night on Broadway. They also found a lot of blood in the back near and inside of a dumpster when they secured the area. Somehow, my gut feeling is telling me that these incidents are all connected.

That's what we need to find out, so get going," Agent Kaplin said getting into his car.

"I'm on it Sir! You can count on me," the agent said running back in the building.

***

Yahnise found a payphone and pulled over. She hoped that it worked because hardly any of the payphones in Philly ever worked anymore because of vandalism. It wasn't a priority for the phone companies to fix the payphones because mostly everyone had cellphones now. She took out some change that she found in the ashtray of the car and jumped out the car. People were looking at her because she had a lot of blood on her and she was practically naked and barefoot. She didn't care about the onlookers though; all she cared about was contacting EJ.

She picked up the phone and it didn't have a dial tone. "NOOOOO! WHY IS THIS HAPPENING TO ME?" she screamed out.

"Miss, are you okay? Do you need me to call the police or anything?" a little girl that was no older than sixteen asked her.

"No, I don't need no cops, but can I please use your phone to call my husband?" she asked the young girl.

"Sure," she said passing her phone to Yahnise.

"Thank you so much. Write your number or address down and I will have something sent to you for helping me," Yahnise said as tears ran down her face.

"That's okay. I don't mind helping you," the young girl said smiling.

Yahnise dialed EJ's cellphone hoping that he would answer.

***

Everyone had made it back to Millick Street without being pulled over. They were sitting in the living room talking. "EJ, I need to speak to you in private for five minutes. This is really important," Sonja said.

EJ remembered that she had said that earlier so he told her to come upstairs because he wanted to know what was on her mind.

When they got upstairs in one of the rooms, EJ shut the door behind them. "What's going on with you? What is so damn important that you need to tell me at a time like this?" he asked.

"I've been trying to tell you that I'm ---," she couldn't finish her statement because once again EJ's phone rang.

He looked at it and held one finger up telling Sonja to hold up for a minutes. He didn't recognize the number, but he was hoping that it was Ed calling to tell him where to meet at so he could get his wife and son back. "Hello! Hello! Who is this?" he said into the phone.

No one had said anything, but he could hear them crying. His heart began to beat fast. "Yahnise, baby is that you?"

"They hurt our baby, EJ! THEY HURT ZIAIRE!" she said, as her crying got louder.

EJ went into straight kill mode. "Who hurt Ziaire, Yahnise? Baby, tell me where you are at. I'm coming to get you. Please calm down and talk to me," he said trying to sound calm.

"I, I, I'm at 33rd and Montgomery. I need you to come get me. I can't drive anymore. They hurt Zi!" she said crying hysterically.

"Don't move baby! I'm on my way! Stay right there! I'm coming!" EJ said running down the steps. "LET'S GO! THEY HURT MY SON!" he screamed when he reached the bottom of the steps.

Everybody jumped up and grabbed their weapons. From the look in EJ's eyes, they already knew somebody was dying today.

***

Yahnise hung up and passed the little girl her phone back. "Do you want me to stay with you just in case you need to make another call?" she asked.

"Thank you, but you've done enough," Yahnise said walking back towards the car. The little girl walked off and went on about her business.

When she opened the car door, the strong order of her dead son hit her like a ton of bricks. His body was already starting to decay and she knew she had to get some help for him, but she was too distraught to do anything. She needed her husband there right now. She sat in the car and started crying again with her head on the steering wheel.

***

EJ and Scrap were in the car together, while another car and two vans full of goons followed closely behind. EJ was zooming through red lights as if he owned the streets. He didn't give a fuck about nothing but getting to his family.

"I'm killing everything moving if they hurt my son real bad!" EJ said while beeping his horn for cars to get out of the way.

"Try to keep a level head man. That's why I'm here, to eliminate all of your fucking problems!" Scrap said making sure the AR-15 was fully loaded.

"That's the fucking reason I still don't have my family back, because I let y'all handle shit instead of doing it myself!"

Scrap just looked out the window. He knew EJ was speaking off of emotions so he just bit his tongue and let him vent.

Neither of the men spoke for the rest of the ride there. As soon as they got to the corner of 33rd and Montgomery, EJ threw the car in park and jumped out with his forty caliber in his hand. He started looking around for his wife and when he saw her getting out of the car, he ran to her.

She started running also and she jumped in his arms. He held her tight in his arms, not wanting to ever let her go. "I'm here baby! I'm here! Everything is going to be okay! I won't let no one hurt you ever again! Where is Ziaire and what happened to him?" he said releasing his hold on her and looking in her eyes.

She broke down crying again. "He, he, he's gone EJ! THEY KILLED MY BABY! THEY KILLED ZIAIRE!"

"Where is my son, Yahnise?" EJ said angrily.

She pointed to the car and EJ took off in that direction. He got to the car and as soon as he seen the bloody sheet, he fell apart.

"NOOOOO! NO! NO! NOT MY SON!"

He didn't even care about the scene he was causing or anybody that was watching. He picked his son up and cradled him like a baby as he cried profusely.

Scrap ran up to him. "Come on man, we have to get the hell out of here! It's too many people watching! The pigs will be here any minute now! I know you're hurting, but we have to bounce!" he said trying to help EJ up.

EJ carried his son back to his car. He and Yahnise jumped in the back, while Scrap drove. Sonja was watching the whole thing and she started crying her eyes out as they left the scene.

***

An hour later, they were all riding around trying to find Ed. EJ had called Nyia and Ms. Pam to come stay with Yahnise. They took Ziaire to a funeral home where they personally knew the owner. He said that he would take care of everything without getting the cops involved.

"Let's check and see if that bitch mom and son are home. If they are, we are going to get a number for Ed and then kill them both," EJ said.

They had went past N.O.B., but it was taped off. EJ didn't want to be nowhere around that, so they left. If he could have seen Shannon and that other nigga, he would have put more lead in their already dead bodies. He was pissed that Shannon had betrayed him like this. He made up his mind that after he killed Ed, he would be officially out of the game. He was going to take Yahnise and move to Miami. They were never coming back to Philly again.

"She still lives on that little block off of 71st and Paschall, right?" Scrap asked.

"Yeah, Theodore Street. Nobody walks out of there, even if they give us all the information we need. It's time to make a mutha-fucking statement!"

They pulled up to Shannon's mom house and EJ jumped out before the car could even stop moving. Scrap and Chris jumped out also. They all headed up the steps and without even a warning, EJ shot the locks off of the door.

BOOM!

BOOM!

"Playtime is up," EJ said as he walked in the door looking for anybody. A man was sitting on the couch watching TV when he heard the shots. He jumped up when he saw EJ and his crew.

"What is thi---," he never got to finish that statement.

BOOM!

BOOM!

BOOM!

EJ sent three shots to his heart, putting him to sleep forever. They walked right pass him, splitting up looking for anybody else that might be in the house.

Shannon's mom was in her bedroom when she heard the shots. She quickly grabbed her phone and dialed 911. Before they could pick up, Chris grabbed the phone from her and ended the call.

"Who else is here with you besides the guy downstairs?" he asked sternly.

She shook her head from side to side. "Nobody else is here, but me and Paul," she said nervously.

He pulled her out the door and down the steps. When they got to the bottom, EJ was waiting for them.

"Sit the fuck in the chair and you better not say a word," EJ said as Scrap and Chris kept their guns aimed at her.

"Now I don't have any time for games or repeating myself. You only get one chance to answer my question and I want the truth. What is Ed's phone number and where is he staying right now? Before you answer, I know that you know because you watch his son for Shannon. After I get my answer, I will leave you alone. Now, please speak up and answer my question," EJ said to her.

She was shaking and scared to death. "His number is 267-386-1523, and he lives on 51st and Spruce on the first floor. I've only been over there twice to pick up my grandson. That is all I know," she said with her voice shaking.

"Okay, where is his son now?"

"He is in daycare," she answered.

"I want you to call Ed right now and tell him that you're going to bring his son to the house in an hour."

Scrap passed her the house phone and she dialed Ed's cell. He picked up on the second ring. "Hello."

"Ed, I'm gonna bring Junior over in an hour. Will you be there?" she said nervously as EJ and his men listened on speakerphone.

"No, I'm on my way to the club. I have a meeting with someone tonight. Why isn't Shannon answering her phone? I've been calling her for the last thirty minutes," he said.

"I don't know. Maybe she turned her ringer off or something. I'll try to call her after I hang up with you," she said.

"She supposed to be at the club keeping an eye on my package. I'm a find out what's going on when I get there. Well, let me get off this phone. I'll have her call you and come get Junior in a little while," Ed said.

Tired of the games, EJ snatched the phone from the lady. "Nigga, before you hang up, there's something you should know. I wouldn't even go to the club, because all you are going to find is a couple of dead bodies and a bunch of pigs there!"

"Ohhhh, so the big man wants to step up and finally go toe to toe with me. You may have gotten to your wife, but you were too late for your son. I can't wait for you to join him, you bitch ass nigga," Ed said laughing.

That only fueled the fire in EJ's eyes. "I thought families were off limits and we are going to see who the real bitch is sooner than you think. I have somebody that you want now," EJ said with aggression in his voice.

"And just who would that be?" Ed asked already knowing the answer to his own question.

"I HAVE YOUR SEED NOW, SO COME GET HIM!" EJ yelled into the phone.

"I didn't kill that spoiled little brat so don't touch my son or you will be dead by morning!" Ed said.

"You didn't have anything to do with it? You kidnapped my wife and son and then my son ends up dead. What's funny is, all this time that I've known you, I never even knew you had a seed. We used to talk about everything and you kept that part of your life from me, so the way I see it, you already had larceny in your heart. It just took Shannon to come along and help bring it out of you. It's okay though, because she got hers and you soon will be getting yours," EJ told him.

"Let's just get this over with. Wherever you want to settle this at, I'm there so just name the place and time," Ed said.

"That old warehouse on 54th and Willows at 10:00 tonight. Just so you know that I mean business! You can say goodbye to your son's grandma!"

BOOM!

BOOM!

EJ put two shots in the woman's skull.

"Ha! Ha! Ha!" Ed laughed. "I never liked the bitch, anyway! I'll be there and by the way, after I shot your wife up with Blood Game, I shot her pussy up with some cum game along with my crew! So when you make love to her for the last time before you die tonight, make sure you let her know that it's you and not me hitting those gushy walls! See you soon bitch boy!" Ed said hanging up.

"That pussy! I'm gonna kill his ass when I catch him! Let's go get his fucking son by any means necessary!" he said as he threw the phone into the wall.

Ed had really got under his skin by hurting his family. Now he knew the inevitable had finally come and it was about to end in blood.

***

They walked into the daycare on 70th and Woodland and went straight to the receptionist desk.

"Hello, how may I help you?" the lady said looking up at the three men standing before her.

"I'm here to pick up my nephew, Edward, Jr.," EJ said. He didn't know what last name he was there under so he didn't say one.

"And your name, Sir?" she asked.

"I'm his uncle and I'm kind of busy so can you hurry this up?"

"Well, I can't release him to you if you are not an authorized family member," she said with a little attitude.

"Look, we can do this the easy way, or the hard way. Either way you want it, is fine with me. I'm still gonna get what I came for," EJ said pulling out his forty caliber.

She tensed up and did exactly what she was told to do. She got up and walked across the hall to retrieve the little boy. He was in the room playing with three other little kids on a mat on the floor. From where they were all standing, the four kids were in plain view. After they got the boy, they made their way towards the door. Chris and the couple of goons that were standing by the door put the little boy in the van and they left the daycare.

EJ didn't do anything to the lady or the other three kids that were still there. He didn't even care if they called the cops. If they interfered with him getting revenge, they would get it too.

CHAPTER 26

War Time

A gent Kaplin was on his way back from the N.O.B. crime scene. He had just talked to the agent at the other crime scene and just as he thought, they were both connected.

The first crime scene looked like someone had been held hostage and somehow they had managed to get away. The evidence showed that a fourth person got out and they were presumed to be hurt very bad. He told his agent to alert every hospital in the surrounding area, that someone may come in with a gunshot wound and to call him if they got any leads from it.

The second crime scene was a slaughterhouse. All four men were executed. They were killed with high caliber weapons. What made them realize that they were both linked was the fact that both places belonged to Ed. He knew this from all the surveillance his team had been collecting. Now it was time to bring this war between the two ex-friends to a close before more innocent people got hurt in the process.

Agent Kaplin made a call to headquarters. As soon as the agent answered the phone, he told him what he needed done.

"I need you to contact our field agent that's on the Johnson and Young case and get the information for us to go in tonight. We have to get these two off the streets now. We can't wait any longer," Agent Kaplin said.

"I'll get right on it. There is something you should know, also. A bunch of men ran up in a daycare on Woodland Avenue and abducted a little boy. They didn't harm anybody else, but guess who the little boy's father is," the agent said.

"Eric or Edward?" Agent Kaplin asked.

"Edwards! From all of our data, I didn't even know he had a child. The locals have already put out an Amber Alert on the child. A few agents are headed over there right now with a forensic specialist. We already know who's behind it, but we still have to go through the proper investigation to cover our asses. I just hope they don't hurt that poor little boy," he said.

"Me too! Why would they want to kidnap him, anyway?" Agent Kaplin asked.

"Oh damn! You didn't hear about what happened earlier. Our field agent told us that Ed's crew kidnapped EJ's wife and son a couple of days ago. His wife was able to get away, but their son wasn't so lucky. They murdered him right in front of his mom," the agent said with disgust.

"That explains everything now. EJ is out for revenge in the form of street justice. We have to get this situation under control now. I want you to put every available man on this now. We have to find that location and fast. Make sure you hit our field agent up and track the phone if you don't get an answer. I know whatever is going happen, it's going to happen tonight," Agent Kaplin said.

"I'll take care of it right now. I'll hit you up as soon as we have an address of where it's going down," he said.

Agent Kaplin hung up the phone and just kept driving hoping that they got there before it was too late.

***

Ed had gathered up about eight niggas that he had on the streets. They were headed for the warehouse to handle their business with EJ once and for all. It was only 9:30, but they wanted to get there first so that they would have the drop on EJ and his team.

"I'm telling everyone now; nobody walks out of there alive unless it's us. That means, I want every last one of them dead," Ed said to his people. They were all riding in a big Ecoline van that one of Ed's men had stolen from around the way. It was enough artillery in there to take on a whole police district.

"Don't worry, no one will be leaving out of there, except in a body bag," one of Ed' men said. He had a street sweeper in his lap making sure it was locked and loaded.

"Just make sure that no one fires a shot until I have my son out of there safe and sound. Once he is safe, I want you niggas to light that mutha-fucka up like the Fourth of July."

Everybody sat in silence until they arrived at the warehouse. The building had been condemned for a few months now, but the lights still worked. Ed ordered his men to take positions throughout the place as they waited for EJ to get there.

***

Chris, EJ, Scrap, and ten niggas were in three GMC Terrains watching Ed and his men hide throughout the building. They watched through the dark tint as they checked their weapons.

"These niggas must really think they're slick, huh? I knew he would try to get here before us, that's why I needed you to get us here an hour early. Make sure this nigga doesn't get away this time. I want to end this tonight. Either he is going to kill me or I'm going to kill him. Make sure everybody had a vest on," EJ said to Scrap and Chris.

"Don't let your emotions get you killed in there. Try relaxing and keep your head in the game. This is not only for your safety, but ours as well," Scrap said.

"I'm with y'all no matter what. Scrap, I just want to apologize in front of everybody here for what I said earlier. We all tried to get this nigga and failed. It pissed me off that he hurt my family, but no matter what happens here, y'all are my peeps," EJ said sincerely to everybody.

"Nigga, if you are done with that emotional shit, let's go kill this nigga so we can get home and finish making money," Scrap said.

"I know cause this soft ass nigga looked like he wanted to shed a tear or something," Chris said. They all started to laugh before getting out the care with Ed's son who was tied up.

All the goons jumped out ready for war with ski mask and black leather gloves on. It was time to get it popping.

A half a block away, the undercover agent had followed them to the warehouse and he was now on his phone informing the other agents what was about to take place.

***

"Okay, gather around. We now have the location and it's about to go down. Our agent said they are at the old warehouse on 54th and Willows in Southwest Philly. I need every available agent on this case. Everyone needs to be geared up with tactical equipment and ready to go in five minutes. Now move!" Agent Kaplin said putting on his Special Weapons and Tactics (SWAT) uniform.

"I'm ready now Sir and I have two tactical teams in route as we speak just in case we don't get there before all hell breaks loose. They should be there in fifteen minutes," Jim said.

"Good thinking, Jim! Now let's hurry up and get there before any more blood is shed," he said heading towards the door.

By the time Jim and Agent Kaplin got down to the garage, there were thirty agents waiting by their cars. They all jumped in their cars and SUV's and headed for Southwest with lights and sirens blaring.

***

"Chris, take a team and go through the back so that we can ambush these niggas form the front and back. Scrap come with me," EJ said.

They walked in the building and headed towards the area that was lit up. As soon as they walked through, Ed and two niggas with assault rifles were standing there.

"I knew you wouldn't come alone. You had to bring your little side kick with you," Ed said.

"What do I look like to you; a fucking fool coming her by myself when you have your little crew all around this place. Give me more credit than that, old friend. I've been around you long enough to know how you move, but I didn't come here to talk and I damn sure didn't come here to make up so what you wanna do?" EJ said gripping his gun tighter.

"First, I want my son and then we can handle this like men."

Scrap had the little boy by the collar while holding the AK-47 waiting to see when EJ would strike.

"Let that nigga go to his dad," EJ said raising the riot pump a little.

Scrap let the little boy go and he started running towards his dad. EJ raised the pump and fired.

BOOM!

Hitting little Ed, Jr. in the back killing him before he hit the ground.

"NOOOO! YOU SON OF A BITCH! KILL THEM MUTHA-FUCKAS!" Ed screamed as guns started firing from everywhere.

EJ and Scrap ducked behind the wall and returned fire. Once the riot pump was empty, EJ pulled his Tech-9 from behind his back and let it go. He hit one of Ed's men in the chest as he came up to fire again.

Two of EJ's goons were coming through the back door when they were met by a barrage of bullets. Their vest took most of the shots until they fell on the ground. They couldn't even get a shot off before two other niggas were up on them empting their clips into their face and bodies.

***

The agents heard all the shots and immediately called for backup. As the first wave of the tactical team arrived, the agents quickly jumped out their cars and ran for the door. "MOVE IN! MOVE IN!" one of the agents yelled to about twenty other agents as they all stormed in the building.

"We're almost there! We'll back you up in less than two minutes! Be careful!" Agent Kaplin said trying to hurry up to help his team.

"FBI! FREEZE! EVERYBODY GET DOWN ON THE GROUND!" one agent screamed.

"DROP YOUR WEAPONS OR DIE!" another agent yelled.

EJ and Scrap were still shooting at Ed and the niggas that were with him when they heard the agents.

"I'm not going back to prison," Scrap said.

"Well then, let's do what we gotta do then," EJ said reloading the Tech-9 and continuing to fire at Ed.

They both started firing on the FBI agents as they came through the door. The five agents that entered, all caught shots to the neck and face. Scrap and EJ knew they were fully armored up so they aimed for their heads. They started running to get out of the line of fire, from both Ed and the agents.

Ed and the goons that were with him started running to get away from the FBI also.

EJ saw them run up the steps and he ran after them. "I'm not leaving here until I get that bitch ass nigga!" he said to Scrap.

"Let's go then," he said chasing after Ed.

EJ and Ed's men were killing FBI agents as they entered the door until they heard about fifteen cars coming to a screeching halt outside and what seemed like fifty more agents started surrounding the building.

"Let's go! We have officer's down! Let's get the wounded out of the line of fire and regroup," Agent Kaplin yelled in the bullhorn.

***

Cops and FBI agents were all over the place outside. They were waiting for the right moment to enter the building. They had retrieved most of the wounded or dead agents. Agent Kaplin was pissed because now he was fighting two different groups of people and he had already lost ten agents. He knew that he had to get this situation under control and fast.

Two helicopters were hovering over the building. Four sharp shooters jumped out and started setting up to take out targets.

"If you get a clear shot, take it!" Agent Kaplin said through the radio. He wanted these dangerous suspects dead, now! Fuck taking them into custody!

***

EJ and Scrap were still chasing Ed and the other shooters. "You go after that nigga while I get Ed's bitch ass," EJ said to Scrap.

"Yo man, let's make it back out of here alive! Be careful!" Scrap said giving EJ a pound before they split up.

EJ started chasing Ed through a part of the building with a bunch of big machines in it.

TAT!

TAT!

TAT!

TAT!

Ed fired at EJ as he jumped in between two machines.

BLOCA!

BLOCA!

BLOCA!

BLOCA!

CLICK!

CLICK!

EJ returned fire until his Tech-9 was empty. He pulled out his two Glock 9mm's and kept firing.

POP!

POP!

POP!

POP!

"I'm going to kill you before the cops get me so stop running," EJ said hiding behind a machine.

"Fuck you nigga! Let's get it!" Ed said firing his AK again.

TAT!

TAT!

TAT!

TAT!

EJ started ducking trying not to get hit. He moved from one spot as he fired to create a diversion.

***

Scrap was in the locker room of the building. He had chased Ed's man in there. He had pulled his Desert Eagle out and pointed it in front of him looking for any surprises. As he passed the first set of lockers, he never saw the dude step out in the opening.

BOC!

BOC!

He caught two shots in his back and fell face first to the floor. He dropped his gun in the process as Ed's man started walking towards him.

"Well, well, well, what do we have here?" the dude asked as he kicked Scrap in the side. "Now let's see who the bitch is!"

The dude didn't know that Scrap was wearing a vest. He also didn't see the 9mm that he had slid from under it. As he got closer to make his kill, Scrap turned over and fired.

BOC!

BOC!

BOC!

BOC!

Hitting the dude four times in his chest. He fell back and hit the ground.

Scrap was in a lot of pain as he got up holding his chest. He grabbed his Desert Eagle off the floor and headed for the door. When he got to the stairs, he headed to the roof trying to get away by climbing over to the next building. As soon as he reached the top, he went out on the roof and he was met by two federal agents.

"FREEZE! FBI! GET ON THE GROUND! DON'T DO IT! DROP THE GUN!" the agent shouted.

Scrap weighed his options for a moment and realized that he wasn't trying to go back to prison for life. He saw an opening and he took it. In one swift motion, he let off two rapid shots.

BOC!

BOC!

Hitting one agent in his neck and missing the other one. The other agent ducked out of the way. He came up to shoot back, but Scrap's head went back and his body fell to the ground, dead on contact. The sharp shooter in the helicopter had put a bullet in Scrap's head.

"One suspect down on the roof! We also need a paramedic up here! We have an officer down!" was all that was heard through every agent's radio.

All the agents outside had already started moving in, killing everybody that didn't surrender. Agent Kaplin led the team looking for EJ and Ed. He didn't want either one of them to get away. They were going to rot behind a prison wall for the rest of their lives if he caught them without killing them.

***

EJ was still searching for Ed in the machine room. No shots were fired so he didn't know where he was.

Ed was able to get behind him. He put the AK down and pulled out his forty caliber. He knew EJ would have on a vest so he had a clip full of hollow tip bullets. "Drop that gun, nigga and turn around! I told you, you weren't built for this war shit, but you still wanted to try to go at me anyway!" Ed said.

EJ dropped his weapon and turned around slowly with his hands to his side. "You're gonna have to kill me, because if I get a chance, I'm going to kill you," EJ said not fazed by the gun that was being pointed at him.

"Oh, I'm gonna kill you! I just wanted to look you in the eyes before I pulled the trigger," Ed said.

FLIPPING NUMBERS 2 – FRIENDS BECOME FOES

"FEDERAL AGENT! DROP THE GUN AND PUT YOUR HANDS UP!" the agent yelled stepping from behind one of the machines standing next to EJ.

He couldn't believe his eyes as he watched Sonja standing there with federal tactical gear on. All this time, she was a federal agent. "WHAT THE FUCK? YOU'RE A FUCKING FED!" EJ said.

"I tried to tell you, but we kept getting interrupted. I never wanted you to find out like this. I was called in from California because they knew that me and Yahnise were best friends and I would be able to get close to you without anybody suspecting anything," Sonja said.

"So you seduced me just to get even closer to me and I was too fucking blind to see it?" EJ said pissed off.

"I'm sorry! I was just doing my job. Now Edward, I need you to drop your weapon and put your hands up," Sonja said aiming her gun at Ed.

"Man, fuck that! I'm gonna die anyway!" he said firing at them.

BOOM!

BOOM!

EJ ducked behind a machine as he saw Sonja take two shots to the chest.

Ed started to move in to finish Sonja off when EJ reached for her gun and fired at Ed hitting him three times causing him to fall and drop his weapon. EJ quickly rushed over to him aiming his gun at his head.

"Go ahead, you bitch ass nigga! What! You scared to finish the job?"

BOC!

BOC!

BOC!

BOC!

BOC!

EJ shot him five times in the face and head and then he spit on his body.

He looked over and saw Sonja laying on the ground squirming from the pain of the hollow tip bullets that entered her body through her vest. EJ walked up to her with his gun still aimed at her.

She looked up at him. "Please, please don't kill me! I'm pregnant with your child. I never meant to hurt your family," she said coughing up blood.

182

"Why did you try to set me up then? You wanted to take away everything that meant something to me by helping to indict me? Look at me though, I'm still standing so fuck you and that baby," he said before putting two bullets in her face.

BOC!

BOC!

He took off her vest and federal agent jacket and put it on. Next, he grabbed her headgear, radio, and other weapons. He already had on all black so he was hoping that he could pass for an agent.

EJ ran out the door and headed down the steps moving fast so he could reach the bottom before anyone noticed him. As soon as he made it to the bottom, tactical teams were all over the place. It looked like a blood bath from all the bodies that were laid out. He made his way through the crowd hoping that none of them was Scrap or Chris.

***

Agent Kaplin and his team were making a sweep of each floor looking for EJ and Ed. "Does anybody have any eyes on the suspects?" he asked in his radio.

"Negative Sir! No sign of them yet, but we will keep looking! Hold on! Wait! We see something up ahead," the agent said. Then he came right back on his radio and said, "We have an agent down and one of the suspects! I repeat we have an agent down and one suspect! The other suspect is still at large somewhere in the building! Be advised that the other suspect is still at large and he may be dressed as an agent!"

"Damn it! What's your location? We are on our way to you! Nobody leaves this place until every agent dead or alive is accounted for!" Agent Kaplin said frustrated.

There was no way that the suspect was going to make it out of there without being spotted by someone. They had the building locked down, so they thought. By the time the call came over the radio, EJ had already slipped through the crowd of officers and stolen one of their cars heading out of the area.

EPILOGUE

A couple of days later, EJ and Yahnise were at the cemetery burying their only son. Cars were lined up all the way out the gates as people paid their respects to EJ and his family.

Yahnise was tightly holding on to EJ because she felt like she was going to pass out. Nyia, Mira, Ms. Pam, and Chris all stood next to them as they watched the casket being lowered into the ground.

Chris had made it out of the building unscathed because as soon as he saw all of the cops and federal agents approaching, he ran and jumped the fence to the train tracks. He saw a cargo train-riding pass and he hopped on it, getting away safely.

After they placed the dirt over the casket, they all started walking back to the limos. After Yahnise and everybody else was inside, EJ shut the door and pulled Chris to the side so they could have a private conversation.

"This shit is finally over man. I'm done with the game, for real this time. I was gonna pass the torch over to Scrap and move to Miami, but he's gone now. I guess my question to you is, do you want the business, or do you and Nyia want to roll with us? No matter what, my wife and I are out of here. I can't put her in danger anymore. We are going to start a new life down there away from all of this. Plus, you know those boys are going to be breaking their necks to find me," EJ said.

"Damn, you're really getting out of the game, huh? I don't want to quit yet, so I accept your offer. When I'm tired of this shit, then and only then will I move out of town like you are doing," Chris said seriously.

"Don't let these streets take you away like they have done to so many others. Be smart and stay ahead of the competition. If you need me for anything, I'm only a phone call away. Savino will know where and when to reach out to me," EJ said as the two shared a brotherly embrace.

"That hug made me feel like we won't see each other again."

"The feds won't stop looking for me because they lost a lot of agents so I have to always be on the move," EJ said.

"That was fucked up that sharing a crib with Yahnise's best friend almost became your downfall. At least you got that bitch. What about that problem with your wife? Will she be okay?" Chris asked.

"Yeah, she's fighting the little urges that keep trying to take over her, but all and all, my baby will be good."

"Well, let's get out of here so y'all can get ready for the big trip tomorrow. Don't worry about the house and stuff, Nyia will sell everything and wire the money to you," Chris said opening the limo door so they could get in.

"EJ, hold up," Erica said walking over to him. "Can I talk to you real quick? It will only take a minute."

"Give me a second, Chris. I'll be right back," EJ said as they walked a few feet away from the limo.

"I just wanted to say sorry for your loss, and if you ever need to talk, just call me. I'm headed back to ATL tonight so I wanted to give you a going away present," she said handing him a picture.

EJ looked down at the picture of Ed, Ms. Cynthia, Erica, and Ed, Jr. What made him become alert was that everybody had a RIP sign above their head except for Erica. Before he could look back up at her, he heard two muffled sounds as his stomach felt hot and wet.

PHHH!

PHHH!

"What are you doing?" he asked dropping down on one knee.

She looked at him with sinister eyes and said, "You took all my family away from me! I didn't care about my mom because she was a rat, and I didn't care that you and my brother were beefing. What I did care about was you killing my nephew. Since you took away the only family I had left, I'm gonna take you away from yours. Goodbye EJ!"

PHHH!

PHHH!

She hit him two more times before running away to the awaiting car and hopping in the passenger seat. The driver sped off heading for the cemetery exit leaving EJ laying on the ground.

Chris and Nyia were so busy comforting Yahnise, that they never saw EJ fall or Erica running to the car until they heard the screeching tires.

"OH SHIT EJ!" Chris yelled jumping out of the limo running after the car trying to get away.

Yahnise looked up and jumped out of the car followed by Nyia. "NOOOOO! NOT AGAIN!" she yelled running over to her husband and dropping down in front of him. She lifted his body up into her arms.

Tears were running down her face like a faucet. "SOMEBODY HELP ME, PLEASE! DON'T YOU DIE ON ME, BABY! I LOVE YOU SO MUCH!"

EJ looked up into her eyes and said, "I love you too," before seeing total darkness…

Featured New Release

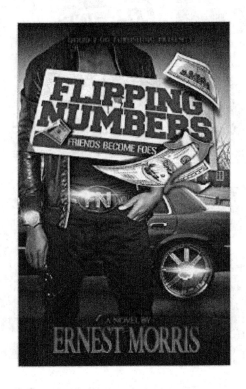

Books by Good2Go Authors on Our Bookshelf

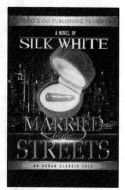

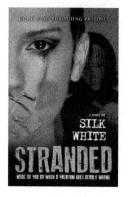

SLUMPED PART 1

JASON BRENT

TEARS OF A HUSTLER

A NOVEL BY

SILK WHITE

TEARS OF A HUSTLER 2

A NOVEL BY

SILK WHITE

GOOD 2 GO PUBLISHING PRESENTS

TEARS OF A HUSTLER 3

A NOVEL BY

SILK WHITE

TEARS OF A HUSTLER 4

YOU'VE BEEN WARNED

A NOVEL BY

SILK WHITE

SILK WHITE

TEARS OF A HUSTLER 5

THE SPADES

GOOD 2 GO PUBLISHING PRESENTS

A NOVEL BY

SILK WHITE

TEARS OF A HUSTLER 6

THE RETURN OF THE WOLF

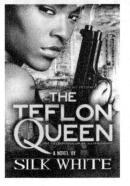

THE TEFLON QUEEN

A NOVEL BY

SILK WHITE

THE TEFLON QUEEN 2

A NOVEL BY

SILK WHITE

Good2Go Films Presents

To order books, please fill out the order form below:

To order films please go to www.good2gofilms.com

Name: _____

Address: _____

City: _____ State: _____ Zip Code: _____

Phone: _____

Email: _____

Method of Payment: Check   VISA   MASTERCARD

Credit Card#: _____

Name as it appears on card: _____

Signature: _____

Item Name	Price	Qty	Amount
48 Hours to Die – Silk White	$14.99		
Flipping Numbers – Ernest Morris	$14.99		
Flipping Numbers 2 – Ernest Morris	$14.99		
He Loves Me, He Loves You Not - Mychea	$14.99		
He Loves Me, He Loves You Not 2 - Mychea	$14.99		
He Loves Me, He Loves You Not 3 - Mychea	$14.99		
Married To Da Streets – Silk White	$14.99		
My Besties – Asia Hill	$14.99		
My Boyfriend's Wife - Mychea	$14.99		
Never Be The Same – Silk White	$14.99		
Stranded – Silk White	$14.99		
Slumped – Jason Brent	$14.99		
Tears of a Hustler - Silk White	$14.99		
Tears of a Hustler 2 - Silk White	$14.99		
Tears of a Hustler 3 - Silk White	$14.99		
Tears of a Hustler 4- Silk White	$14.99		
Tears of a Hustler 5 – Silk White	$14.99		
Tears of a Hustler 6 – Silk White	$14.99		
The Panty Ripper - Reality Way	$14.99		
The Teflon Queen – Silk White	$14.99		
The Teflon Queen 2 – Silk White	$14.99		
The Teflon Queen – 3 – Silk White	$14.99		
The Teflon Queen 4 – Silk White	$14.99		
Time Is Money - Silk White	$14.99		
Young Goonz – Reality Way	$14.99		
Subtotal:			
Tax:			
Shipping (Free) U.S. Media Mail:			
Total:			

Make Checks Payable To: Good2Go Publishing - 7311 W Glass Lane, Laveen, AZ 85339

CPSIA information can be obtained at www.ICGtesting.com
Printed in the USA
LVOW04s0035150615

442424LV00029B/647/P